This Igloo book belongs to:

..............................................

*Published in 2012*
*by Igloo Books Ltd*
*Cottage Farm*
*Sywell*
*Northants*
*NN6 0BJ*
*www.igloobooks.com*

*Copyright © 2012 Igloo Books Ltd*

*GOS001 0712*
*10 9 8 7 6 5 4 3 2 1*
*ISBN: 978-0-85780-632-1*

*Printed and manufactured in China*

# Stories
## for Girls

igloobooks
.com

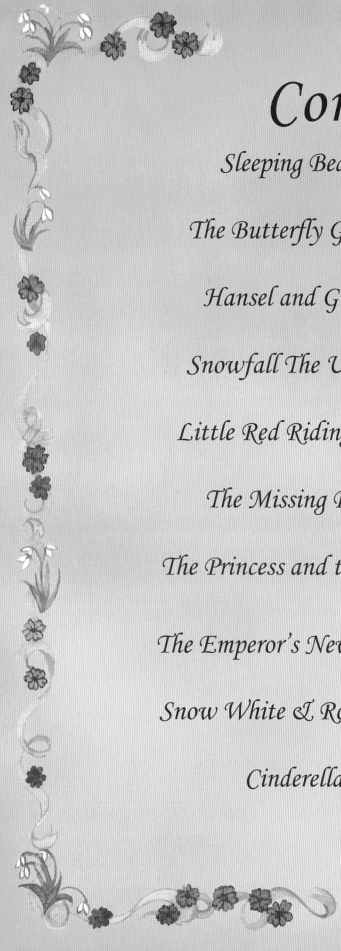

# Contents

# Sleeping Beauty

O nce upon a time, a baby girl was born to a king and queen. She looked so bright and fair, they decided to name her, 'Beauty' and a great celebration was held in her honour.

Because the queen was half-fairy, she invited three of her fairy cousins to give blessings to the baby. However, she forgot to invite one distant relative – a fairy with a very bad-temper.

On the day of the blessings, the fairies gathered round the child's crib. "I give Beauty the gift of goodness and kindness," said the first fairy. "I give Beauty the gift of graceful dancing," said the second fairy.

However, before the third fairy could utter her blessing, a cold wind whirled around the crib. The angry fairy, who had not been invited, appeared. Her face was like thunder. "So, you're having a christening without me?" she snarled, "Now this child will have my present, whether you like it or not! I curse Beauty to prick her finger on her sixteenth birthday and die!" Suddenly, the wind whirled again and the fairy vanished.

Everyone was too shocked to speak. Finally, the third fairy spoke. "I have not given my gift yet," she said in a small voice. "It is not within my power to lift the curse laid on Beauty, but I can change it a little. My gift to you, Beauty, is this – you will not die on your sixteenth birthday, but you will sleep for a hundred years, until you are awakened by true love's first kiss."

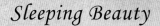

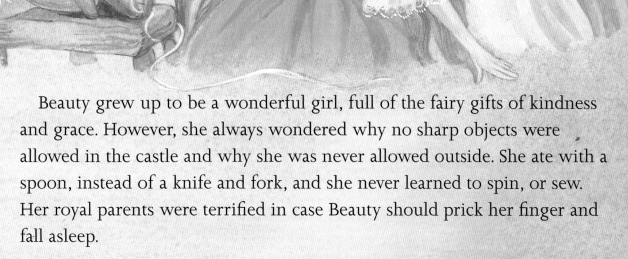

Beauty grew up to be a wonderful girl, full of the fairy gifts of kindness and grace. However, she always wondered why no sharp objects were allowed in the castle and why she was never allowed outside. She ate with a spoon, instead of a knife and fork, and she never learned to spin, or sew. Her royal parents were terrified in case Beauty should prick her finger and fall asleep.

On the day of her sixteenth birthday, Beauty was exploring the castle. In one corner of the hall, she saw a little door that she had never noticed before. It led up a winding staircase, to a room in the highest tower of the castle. There, Beauty saw a woman sitting by a spinning wheel.

Beauty greeted the woman and asked what she was doing. "I'm spinning," replied the woman, who was the angry fairy in disguise. "Would you like to try spinning, my child?"

"Yes, please," said Beauty and she sat at the spinning wheel.
The fairy passed Beauty a sharp spindle, to wind the thread. Beauty took it
but, as she did, she pricked her finger. Instantly, Beauty slumped onto a dusty
old bed and fell into a deep, sleep.

As soon as Beauty began to sleep, a strange thing happened in the castle.
The king and queen, on their thrones, yawned and dozed off. The court jester
slumped to the floor and the cook fell asleep in the middle of preparing
dinner. Soon, everyone in the castle had drifted off to sleep.

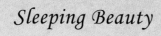

Around the castle moat, green tendrils began to sprout from the ground. In moments, the tendrils grew up and up and twined their way around the castle. Huge, sharp, thorns grew thickly. It was part of the third fairy's magic, to protect Beauty and the castle from harm.

When people in the outside world saw what had happened to the castle, they stayed away. Occasionally, an adventurer would come, seeking the riches of the sleeping king, but they were always turned back by the sharp thorns and the castle remained untouched.

One hundred years passed in silence, until a handsome prince rode by. He had stumbled upon the thorn-covered castle. "I must find out what is inside," said the prince. He drew his sword and cut straight through the thick tangle of thorns.

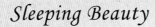

The prince soon found himself inside the huge castle. Everywhere he looked, there were sleeping people – the guards at the gate, the court jester snoring in the hall, even lords and ladies, lying on the great stairs. Everything was covered with cobwebs. The prince tried to wake the sleeping people, but they just murmured and went back to sleep.

As he passed through the Great Hall, the prince saw a little door standing open. It led to a tiny, winding staircase. Climbing the staircase, he found a room in the highest tower of the castle, with an old, cobwebbed spinning wheel, standing in one corner. On the dusty bed, lay the most beautiful girl he had ever seen. He leaned over and gave the girl a single kiss. Beauty stirred and opened her eyes. When she saw the prince, she fell instantly in love.

The spell was broken and the silent castle began to stir. The king and queen woke up, the jester started to juggle and the cook began cooking. The whole castle had come back to life. The prince went to the king and asked him for his daughter's hand in marriage.

In no time at all, the people of the castle had recovered from their hundred years' sleep. The prince and Beauty were married and everyone lived happily ever after.

# The Butterfly Garden

Lottie, Sam and Michelle were the best of friends. One day, just before school ended for the summer, they were wandering home along the lane that led to their road, when all at once they stopped. Dancing in front of them was the most beautiful butterfly they had ever seen.

"It's so pretty!" whispered Sam. "I wish I was a butterfly."

Another butterfly appeared, then another, and another. There were butterflies everywhere. The three girls watched, enchanted, as the gentle creatures swirled around them then fluttered back up the lane.

"Let's follow them!" cried Lottie, grabbing her friends' hands.

The girls followed the fluttering trail through the park and into the town, until they came to a door in a wall behind the bus stop. The door was slightly ajar.

"Do you think we should follow them?" whispered Michelle.

"Absolutely!" cried Lottie. She grabbed hold of her friends once again and pulled them through before they could protest.

The girls stepped out into a sun-drenched public garden.

"Oh!" gasped Sam. "It's beautiful!"

The velvety lawn was divided by archways dripping with flowers. Right in the middle was a pond with a fountain. Everywhere the girls looked, there were butterflies and other creatures. Birds sang and dragonflies hummed as the girls wandered along the walkways, breathing in the scent of a thousand flowers.

# The Butterfly Garden

It was only when they reached the fountain that Lottie found her voice. "I don't think I've ever been anywhere as beautiful as this. I can't believe it was just sitting here in the middle of town all this time."

The girls sat in the garden and looked around for a long time, until their tummies began to rumble and they remembered it was nearly time for supper. Only then did they reluctantly go home.

Lottie, Sam and Michelle visited the garden almost every day that summer. They had picnics, played games, and chatted while watching the butterflies dance around. It was their secret.

One Sunday, towards the end of the summer, Sam was having lunch with her family when something in the conversation made her sit up and pay attention. Sam's dad was talking about a new shopping mall that was going to be built in the middle of town. As she listened, it slowly dawned on Sam where they were planning to build it. They were going to build it right on top of the garden. The news upset Sam so much, she could barely finish her lunch. Afterwards she ran upstairs to her room and burst into tears.
Their beautiful secret garden was going to be destroyed. It was more than she could bear.

# The Butterfly Garden

Later that day Sam met her friends at the garden as usual, and told them the terrible news.

"We've got to do something!" cried Lottie. "This must be why the butterflies led us here, so that we could save their garden!"

"But what can we do?" asked Michelle. "Who will listen to us?"

Lottie was adamant. "We have to try. We can't let it be destroyed."

All afternoon, the girls discussed ways to save the garden. They felt sure that if others knew how wonderful it was, then maybe they could convince the town council to save it.

"I know," said Lottie. "Why don't we organize a party at the garden?"

"Great idea!" the others agreed. "Then everyone can see how special it is."

The girls spent the rest of the week making invitations, which they mailed to everyone they could think of: friends, parents, teachers – even the mayor.

When the day of the party arrived, the girls spent the whole morning preparing food and drinks for their guests. They borrowed chairs and tables and arranged them around the garden.

Finally they hung banners from the trees that said "Save the Butterfly Garden!"

As the guests arrived, the three friends showed them around, and told them about the shopping mall.
"We must save the garden!" they explained. "It doesn't just belong to the town. It belongs to all the creatures that live here too."

Everybody who saw the garden agreed that it had to be saved, and they all signed a petition. Soon the girls had over one hundred signatures. At the end of the afternoon, the girls approached the mayor, who was sitting admiring the fountain.
"Excuse me," said Lottie nervously. "We'd like to present you with our petition to save this garden."
"Thank you," said the mayor kindly, "but I'm afraid that the plans have already been approved. I'm sorry, but the decision is out of my hands at this stage. So, girls, unless you can come up with a miracle, this wonderful garden will be knocked down." And with a sad smile the mayor left.

The girls were devastated. They sat in a corner, unable to believe that they had failed, even with all the signatures and hard work they had put in.
"Never mind," consoled Sam's father. "Maybe there's something else you can do to save the garden. But right now we need to tidy up this mess."
The three girls started to clear up all the leftovers.
"It's not fair," sighed Michelle, gazing at a blue butterfly, sitting on the rim of a cup she was holding. "Why are buildings more important than a beautiful butterfly like this?"

# The Butterfly Garden

Lottie turned to look. A strange expression came over her face.
"Don't move, Michelle," she whispered. "Sam! Quick! Bring me
my camera. I think that butterfly is a Cornhill Beauty. It's a very rare species.
I saw one in my wildlife book the other day."

Sam and Michelle held their breath as Lottie held up the camera and fiddled
with the lens. SNAP! She just managed to take a picture before the butterfly
fluttered away.

"I think we might just have found our miracle," cried Lottie, grinning from
ear to ear. "We can e-mail this picture to the Science Museum. Cornhill
Beauties are a protected species!"

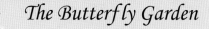

*The Butterfly Garden*

The girls waited anxiously all the following day for a reply to their email. "Maybe they didn't get it!" suggested Sam, after they had checked their in-box for the hundredth time that afternoon. "Let's send it again." Suddenly, the computer went ding.

"We've got mail!" cried Lottie, clicking on her in-box. The three girls eagerly crowded around the computer screen.

"It's from the Science Museum," read Sam. "It is a Cornhill Beauty. The head zoologist wants to come and see the garden for himself. He says that if Cornhill Beauties really live there, it must be a protected habitat. The shopping mall will have to be built somewhere else. He is going to speak to the planning department at the town hall right away."

And that's exactly what happened. It wasn't long before the local newspapers were full of the story about Lottie, Michelle and Sam, and how they had saved the garden from demolition. The girls even received a letter from the mayor, thanking them for all their hard work.

# The Butterfly Garden

"Our garden is going to be renamed," said Lottie, as she read the letter out loud. It's going to be called The Butterfly Garden."

Now the whole town enjoys The Butterfly Garden. But nobody loves it more than Lottie, Sam and Michelle. To this day, they hold a party there every summer, to celebrate its rescue, and to remind everyone how just how special it is.

# Hansel and Gretel

O nce upon a time, there was a boy named Hansel and his sister, Gretel. They lived with their father and their stepmother in a little house deep in the forest. The family were poor and there were many days when they had nothing to eat.

One night, the stepmother said to their father, "We have no food for the children. I will take them to my sister's house, where they will be better fed." However, the stepmother secretly wanted to get rid of Hansel and Gretel. She planned to take them in the forest and leave them there.

The next morning, the stepmother gave Hansel and Gretel some bread for their lunch and led them out into the woods. Hansel, who was clever, guessed that something was wrong. When the stepmother wasn't looking, he tore up his bread and scattered it behind him as they walked.

The stepmother made Hansel and Gretel walk a very long way. When they became tired, she told them to sleep under a tree. However, while the brother and sister were sleeping, the stepmother left and returned home.

When Hansel and Gretel woke up, they found they were all alone. It was cold and dark. "Don't worry," said Hansel. "All we have to do is follow my trail of bread crumbs back to our cottage."

But when they went to look for the trail, the children couldn't find it anywhere. The birds of the forest had eaten every single bread crumb, so Hansel and Gretel had no way to get back home.

Hours passed and the children became more and more lost. They had wandered deep into the forest, when they saw a little house in a clearing.

The house was strange and wonderful. Hansel and Gretel had never seen anything like it. The walls were made of gingerbread, the windows were gumdrops, the door was chocolate and the chimney was a big candy cane.

The brother and sister were so hungry that they rushed up to the house and broke off a large chunk of gingerbread. They ate it ravenously and it tasted delicious.

All of a sudden, the chocolate door flew open. An ugly old woman came rushing out. "You naughty children," she cried. "I'll teach you to eat my house." The woman grabbed Hansel and Gretel with her bony hands and dragged them inside, locking the chocolate door behind them.

The woman was a witch. She pushed Hansel into a cage that hung from the ceiling. "I'll be able to keep an eye on you up there," she said. Then the witch made Gretel do the cleaning. "You cannot go to bed until my house is spotless," she cackled. "However, if you do a good job, you will both get lots of sweets to eat."

Just as she promised, the witch gave Hansel and Gretel lots of sweets to eat. At first, the children liked it, but soon they felt sick from eating sweet, sticky sugar all day and they longed for a simple piece of bread.

Each day, the witch would feel Hansel's finger through the bars of his cage and mutter to herself, "Not yet, not yet." Then she would make Hansel eat even more sweets, but the witch never told either of the children why.

One night, Gretel heard the witch mumbling in her sleep. "Mmm, delicious! Hansel, for my supper!" Gretel realized why the witch was feeding Hansel so much candy. She was fattening him up so she could eat him for her dinner!

Gretel told Hansel about the evil plan. So, the next time the witch felt Hansel's finger through the bars, to see if he was fat enough to eat, Hansel stuck a twig out instead. The witch couldn't see very well, so she didn't notice. "Too skinny!" she croaked. "I won't eat you today!"

Even though the witch fed Hansel more and more sweets, he always held out the twig. "Your brother is very strange," said the witch to Gretel, one day. "However much he eats, he never gets any fatter. I think I'll roast him and gobble him up as a snack!"

The witch forced Gretel to light the huge old oven in the corner of the gingerbread house. Because Hansel wasn't fat enough for a proper supper, the witch decided to eat both children together. "Be a good girl and get in the oven and see if it's hot enough yet," said the witch, slyly. When Gretel was inside, the witch planned to close the door and roast her.

But Gretel was as clever as her brother. Instead of getting into the oven, she said, "That's funny. It doesn't seem to be warm at all." "Nonsense," said the witch. "Stand aside and let me see." And the witch climbed all the way into the hot oven.

Quick as a flash, Gretel slammed the door of the big oven and trapped the witch inside. She ran to Hansel and unlocked his cage. They were so happy to be back together again, they hugged each other as if they would never let go. "Quick!" said Gretel, "we must run!"

Before they left, Hansel went upstairs to the witch's room and searched it. Soon he found what he was looking for – a map of the forest. He ran back downstairs, flung open the chocolate door and the two children escaped.

With the help of the map, Hansel and Gretel soon found their way home. In their little house, they found their father crying. He had missed Hansel and Gretel so much. When they told him that the stepmother had abandoned them, their father sent her away forever. And Hansel, Gretel and their father lived happily ever after.

# Snowfall the Unicorn

Far away, where the mountains meet the sea, there is a kingdom of great beauty. Mountains glisten with snowy tops and rivers cascade through green meadows filled with wild flowers. Neither man nor beast wants for anything.

But this was not always so. One year, springtime didn't bring the usual rains, and by summer the air was heavy with heat. It grew hotter and hotter, and the earth became cracked and parched. There was no harvest that year.

By late autumn, the King called together his most trusted advisors to discuss what could be done.
"My wise men, what suggestions do you have," asked the King,
"for I fear my people will starve."
"A rain dance perhaps, your majesty? Maybe we have upset the gods," answered one advisor. The dancer was summoned, but no rains came.

The King once again called together his advisors.
"My wise men, what shall we do?" the king asked.
"Our food stocks are almost empty and my people are thirsty."
"Your majesty we could divert the great river from the north of the kingdom to provide water for everyone, suggested another.

So they journeyed to the north, but when they arrived the great river had dried up and disappeared.

# Snowfall the Unicorn

Winter came, yet the terrible heat continued. Many of the people bade farewell to their homes and set off to other kingdoms in search of food and water.

On Christmas Eve, Princess Natasha, the King's youngest daughter, gazed sadly out of her bedroom window. In the moonlight she could see the dry and parched kingdom. Tears ran down her cheeks as she looked at the wretched landscape.
"Will we ever see snow again?" she whispered to herself. "If only I could do something to save the kingdom. But what can a little girl like me do?
Princess Natasha glanced up into the evening sky, where a lone star was twinkling.
 "Please, bring back the snow," she whispered.
The star twinkled even more brightly. Again she pleaded with the star, "Please, bring back the snow to our poor kingdom."
The star twinkled at her once more, and seemed to move. So Natasha put on her cloak and decided to follow it. She didn't know what else she could do.

The princess followed the bright star. She walked for hours through the dusty fields until she came to the dried-up forest. There, in the middle of a clearing, surrounded by withered trees, she found a unicorn bound with thick rope. "You poor creature!" she cried, kneeling beside the beast. "Who could have done such a thing?"

The unicorn was very still, but when Natasha stroked its back it opened its eyes and looked at her sadly. "Don't worry," said Princess Natasha. "I shall help you." And she set about loosening the ropes, until eventually the unicorn was free.

## Snowfall the Unicorn

As the magical creature rose from the ground something caught Natasha's eye, a tiny white speck floated down from the sky and landed gently on her nose. It was a snowflake!

Soon snowflakes were swirling all around them.
"Thank you, Princess Natasha," said the unicorn. "My name is Snowfall. I control the seasons and bring the winter snow, but I was captured by a band of hunters who tied me up. Unless I am free I have no magical powers."

The snow continued to fall all around them as the unicorn knelt before the princess and offered his back to take her home. And as they rode through the forest something magical happened. With each step they took the trees started to turn green and the grass sprang from the earth once more. Soon the air was filled with the sound of birdsong and forest creatures scurried among the growing hedgerows.

# Snowfall the Unicorn

Finally they reached the King's castle, bringing with them the beautiful snow.

It was the best Christmas gift anyone could ever ask for. When the King heard what had happened he begged Snowfall to stay at the palace so they could keep him safe. And so it came to be that the unicorn lived in the castle garden, and Natasha visited him every day.

Ever since that time, the long summer days are once again filled with bright sunshine, and when winter comes the land is always covered in a blanket of pure white snow. And every Christmas the people look up at the stars twinkling above them, and it reminds them of the terrible year when the unicorn was captured. And they give thanks to the beautiful creature who once again roams free.

# Little Red Riding Hood

Once upon a time, a little girl lived in a cottage with her mother, near the edge of a big, dark wood. She had a lovely, bright red cape with a hood and the little girl wore it so often, everyone called her, "Little Red Riding Hood."

One day, news reached the cottage that Little Red Riding Hood's grandmother was ill. So, her mother gave her a basket of delicious cakes to take to Granny. "Now, listen carefully," said Little Red Riding Hood's mother. "Remember to stay on the path that goes through the woods. You must not stop to pick flowers and don't talk to any strangers on the way."

The woods were deep and dark, even in the middle of the day, but Little Red Riding Hood wasn't scared. Even though she could see the beautiful flowers that grew along the side of the path, she obeyed her mother and did not stop to pick any of them. What Little Red Riding Hood did not know was that, deep in the shadowy trees, a wolf was watching her.

The wolf slunk out of the trees, swishing its bushy tail. "Who are you and where are you going, little girl?" he said.

Little Red Riding Hood had never seen a wolf before, so she wasn't scared. She forgot what her mother had told her about talking to strangers. "My name is Little Red Riding Hood," she said. "I'm off to visit my grandmother who lives on the other side of the wood."

"Really? How very interesting," said the wolf. "You should pick your grandmother some pretty flowers."
"But my mother told me to stay on the path," said Little Red Riding Hood.

"It's very rude to go visiting someone without any flowers," said the wolf. "Anyway, I must be going now, goodbye." With that the wolf slunk off, back into the forest, as if he had never been there at all.

"How strange," thought Little Red Riding Hood. She continued on her way, but she couldn't help thinking about what the wolf had said. "Maybe Granny would like some flowers," she thought.

Further along the path, Little Red Riding Hood noticed some particularly pretty blooms. She couldn't resist any longer and left the path to pick some to give to her grandmother.

There were so many beautiful flowers to choose from, Little Red Riding Hood didn't realize how much time it was taking her. A long time passed before she had collected a perfect bouquet

"Hello," said a voice. It made Little Red Riding Hood jump. She turned to see a woodcutter, who was carrying an axe. "It's getting late," said the woodcutter. "You shouldn't be on your own in the wood."

Little Red Riding Hood told the woodcutter all about her journey. "Best be on your way then," he said, kindly. "Your grandmother will be waiting for you."

Meanwhile, the wolf had run all the way to Little Red Riding Hood's grandmother's house. He knocked on the door and spoke with a high, girlish voice. "Hello, Granny, it's Little Red Riding Hood, can I come in?"

Grandmother got out of bed, hobbled to the door and unlocked it. The nasty wolf grabbed hold of poor Granny, tied a handkerchief round her mouth and pushed her into a cupboard. Then the cunning wolf put on some of Granny's clothes and got into bed.

A while later, Little Red Riding Hood finally reached her grandmother's house. She knocked on the door. "Hello, Granny, it's Little Red Riding Hood, can I come in?"

"Yes, of course, my child," said the wolf, in his best grandmother's voice.

Little Red Riding Hood came in and went over to the bed. "You must excuse my voice," said the wolf, with the sheets drawn right up to his chin. "I've been so ill, it's made me quite hoarse. Come over here and sit on the bed, my dear."

Little Red Riding Hood sat on the bed and looked at the wolf.
"Oh, Granny, what big ears you have," she said.
"All the better to hear you with," said the wolf.

Little Red Riding Hood leaned in a little bit closer. "Oh, Granny, what big eyes you have."

"All the better to see you with," said the wolf.

Little Red Riding Hood began to feel there was something wrong. She looked at the wolf's paws holding the sheet. "Oh, Granny, what big hands you have."

"All the better to hug you with," said the wolf.

Little Red Riding Hood leaned in closer still, to get a better look. "Oh, Granny, what big teeth you have."

"All the better to EAT you with!" cried the wolf, as he sprang out of the bed

But Little Red Riding Hood was a lot faster than her poor grandmother and she jumped out of the way just in time. The wolf chased her round and round the bed. Suddenly, there was a knock at the door. Little Red Riding Hood ran over and flung the door open. Outside, stood the woodcutter.

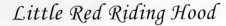

The woodcutter had decided to check on Little Red Riding Hood and her grandmother, to make sure that they were safe. The moment he saw the wolf, the woodcutter swung his axe and chased the nasty creature out of the house and into the dark wood. The wolf got such a fright, he ran away and never came back again.

Little Red Riding Hood let her poor old granny out of the cupboard. She made a drink and Granny, the woodcutter and Little Red Riding Hood ate some of the delicious cakes from the basket. After that, Little Red Riding Hood promised never to stray from the path, ever again.

# The Missing Pony

Gemma was stuck on the second level of her computer game.
"You're not still playing that, are you?" said her mother, coming
into her bedroom. "It's such a lovely day out. Why don't you get some fresh air
instead?"

Gemma groaned. Her mother was always nagging her to get some fresh air, but
the truth was that she hated going out lately because that meant walking past
the empty field by the side of the house.

The field hadn't always been empty. Two months ago it had been home to Merry, a
beautiful little roan pony, but a horse thief had come along one winter's night, and now the
pony was gone.

Tears stung Gemma's eyes, but she refused to cry any more. She looked back at
the computer screen; try as she might, she just couldn't get onto the next level,
so a break might not be such a bad thing. She went down the stairs and gave a soft whistle.

In a flash of brown and white, her little terrier, Benji, came charging at her, wagging his
tail furiously. A walk might cheer her up. Gemma and Benji headed to the place they always
went, a smooth flat rock at the top of the hill that overlooked the town. There was hardly
ever anyone around at this time of day, so she could let Benji run around freely and
let her thoughts drift. And today, as usual, her thoughts drifted to Merry. She
missed her little pony so much. She missed riding her and nuzzling
her neck.

## The Missing Pony

Gemma was lost in her thoughts when the sound of Benji yapping and tearing off down the opposite side of the hill made her snap out of it. In the distance Gemma could make out a figure coming from the woods on that side, heading towards her with Benji jumping around her feet. Benji, who didn't like strangers, never behaved this way, especially since Merry had been stolen.

As the figure got closer she saw the girl scoop the little dog into her arms. She was worried until she recognized who it was – Mary Donnolly, a girl she knew a little from school.

Although Gemma and Mary were in the same class, the girls didn't know each other very well at all. Gemma's friends all thought that Mary was a bit strange and avoided her. It was true that Mary was a little different from the other girls. She wore slightly odd clothes, and she was always on her own, reading books about plants and animals. When you did speak to her she didn't talk about ordinary things like phones or downloads, and Gemma guessed she was the sort of person who liked to be alone. Some of the other girls joked that Mary could do magic, but Gemma thought that was mean, so she always gave her a smile when they passed in the corridor.

# The Missing Pony

As she walked up the hill with the runaway terrier tucked under her arm, Mary recognized Gemma as one of the popular girls at school. She was pretty, wore trendy clothes, and had a lot of friends who were also popular. But unlike the other girls, who nudged each other and whispered as Mary walked past, Gemma had always seemed kind.

As the classmates drew closer they smiled shyly, but when Mary handed over the little dog she wondered why she saw such sadness in Gemma's eyes. "What's wrong?" she asked. "You look like you're missing something."

Gemma was startled by Mary's keen observation. "I'm thinking about my missing pony," she replied without thinking. Mary gave an understanding nod, but Gemma blushed. Why had she shared her secret with someone she hardly knew?
"Bye for now," she smiled awkwardly, turning to leave.
"See you at school." As Mary headed down the hill she was lost in thought. She could not forget the sadness in Gemma's eyes. "I must do my best to help her," she whispered.

When she got home, Mary went straight to her herb garden and picked a sprig
of sweet-smelling rosemary.

"For remembrance," she smiled, as she put it in her basket. Next she picked
lucky lavender, and a handful of dandelions puffballs. As she did this Mary
thought about the girls at school, and how surprised they'd be to know that
some of the things they whispered about her were true – sort of. She wasn't
magic, of course. But she was different; she had a special gift. She used natural
remedies to cure sick animals. And there was something else, too, which she
couldn't quite explain. When she made wishes, they sometimes came true. She
knew the others at school found her odd and shy, and this made her unpopular.
But she didn't know how to change things. And no amount of wishing for
friends of her own seemed to help.

Her wishes only seemed to work for others . . .

That evening, Mary wove the rosemary and lavender into a ring around a pot,
and put the dandelions in the middle. Then she sat down to think about Gemma
and her lost pony. Mary held up the pot in the moonlight and gently blew. The
dandelion seeds drifted away on the cool night breeze as Mary made a wish.

In a nearby valley a little roan pony was falling asleep in his stall when the cool night breeze stirred him. He sniffed and began to wake up. His new owners worked him so hard that he was always so tired these days, but suddenly he felt he could shake off his exhaustion. He was restless.
He started to paw the floor, then he started to kick the door. Finally he used his hind legs to smash the door off its hinges, and he ran out into the night. There was somewhere else he was supposed to be; he remembered that now, and finally he was going home.

Gemma never knew how her beloved Merry came to be whinnying under her bedroom window that night. She never found out where he had been or who had taken him. But she didn't really care. She only cared that he was home and her heartache was over.

But there was one thing about the day her pony came home that nagged at her. When she had locked eyes with strange little Mary Donnelly on the hillside she had seen compassion and wisdom, but also something else; loneliness.

Gemma nuzzled Merry's soft, velvety nose and hugged her silky, smooth neck, then leaped up onto her newly saddled back. As they headed off towards the woods, Gemma urged Merry into a trot and called for Benji to catch up. "Come on boy," she called to the little dog.
"We're off to make a new friend."

# The Princess and the Swan

Once upon a time, a beautiful princess married the handsome prince of a high mountain kingdom. However, after the wedding ceremony, the prince said to the princess, "I cannot stay with you at night. Every evening, I must leave our palace. However, every morning, I will return." The princess was surprised and upset. "Why do you do this?" she asked.

"Please do not ask," said the prince, "I can never tell you."

The prince made the princess promise that whatever happened, she must never follow him." The danger is too great," he said. At first, the princess said she would follow the prince anywhere, but the prince begged her to promise not to. Eventually, the princess relented. "I love you," she said, "and to love is to trust."

So that night, the prince left the palace and the princess wept into her pillow. The next morning, the prince returned, just as he had promised and they spent a wonderful day together. But the next night, the prince left again, and the princess was all alone until morning.

This continued for many months, until the princess could bear it no longer. One night, she secretly watched the prince walk off in the direction of an enormous lake, which lay in the hollow between two great mountains. "I cannot follow him, or I will break my promise," thought the princess. "But what if he is in danger and needs my help?"

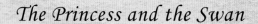

The very next night, the princess found herself creeping down the palace stairs, after the prince, to see where he went. She followed him up hills and down valleys, through woods and fields, until he arrived at a black, marshy lake. There was an island in the middle of the lake, that gleamed silver in the moonlight. On the island was a tall man, in silver robes. Many beautiful white swans surrounded the island. The man raised his arms and the prince seemed to shrink and grow smaller and darker. In a moment, the prince was gone and in his place was a graceful, black swan.

The swan took to the water and the man on the island shouted, "Dance, swans! Follow the prince, your leader, as you must do every night!"

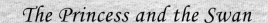

At his command, the swans began to cross the lake in slow, sweeping movements, with the black swan in the lead. The man on the island laughed and sat down to watch.

The swans danced in the water, until the sun began to rise across the mountains. The princess left quickly, so as not to be seen. She saw a single tear, drop from the black swan's eye.

Back at home, the princess didn't know what to do, so she consulted a wise woman who lived near the palace. "The man on the island is a wicked enchanter," said the wise woman. "He has cursed your husband, who must dance for the enchanter every night. The only thing you can do to break the curse, is to destroy the wizard's heart. But it will be hard, because he keeps the heart in a diamond and the diamond is at the very bottom of the lake."

The princess was very frightened, but she knew what she had to do. The very next night, she waited until the prince had departed for the lake and she set out after him. Once the swans began their eerie dance, she knew she had to act. The princess dived into the water, to get the diamond, but the enchanter saw her and cast a magic spell that pulled her towards him.

"So, this is your wife," he said to the black swan. "Because she has broken her promise to you, your curse is doubled. You will be a swan forever!"

The princess cried in shame, but the black swan looked at her and said, "I forgive you. You loved me so much that you wanted to save me. Now, dive again, quickly."

The black swan turned to the enchanter and ran at him, pecking at him with its sharp beak and beating him with its wide wings. The enchanter cried out with rage. He turned from the swan and tried to grab the princess but, quick as a flash, she plunged into the lake and was soon out of his reach.

Holding her breath, the princess dived down and down, into the murky depths. Suddenly, she was something glinting on the bottom of the lake.

The enchanter's heart was inside a gleaming diamond. Grabbing it, the princess swam back up, as fast as she could. She reached the surface and with all her might, the princess crushed the diamond in her hand.

There was a cracking noise and the diamond shattered. Instantly, the enchanter turned into a cloud of silver smoke that blew harmlessly away. The black swan shimmered and grew, until the prince was standing by the princess' side once more. She rushed into his arms and they held each other. When the princess let go of the prince, she saw that they were surrounded by men and women, all dressed in white.

"These were the other swans," explained the prince. "They are my loyal servants from my palace. The enchanter cursed them to stay here forever and he would have killed them all if I had not returned every night to dance with them. But now the curse is lifted and we are all free."

It was a joyous company that walked back to the castle that day.
Finally, the prince and his servants were free from the spell of the enchanter.
As for the enchanter, he was never seen again and the prince and princess
lived happily ever after.

# The Emperor's New Clothes

A long time ago, there lived an emperor who loved clothes more than anything else. Instead of trying to care for his people, he spent all the kingdom's money on fine, new garments. And there was nothing the emperor liked more than parading his new clothes in front of everyone, so they could say how elegant he looked.

One day, two cunning thieves arrived at the emperor's palace. "This silly emperor loves clothes so much," they agreed, "it will be easy to make him shower us with gold." So the thieves went to the emperor and introduced themselves. "We are the finest tailors in the world," they said. "We will make you the best suit of clothes that there has ever been."

At first, the emperor didn't believe them. "I have seen all the finest clothes the world has to offer," he said. "What can you two do that is better than what I have seen already?"

"We have a roll of magic cloth," they said. "It has the finest colors and patterns you have ever seen. It is so exquisite that only the cleverest, most refined people can see it. It is invisible to anyone who is incredibly stupid, or who does not deserve to be doing his job."

"That sounds marvellous," said the emperor, clapping his hands. "If I have a suit of this material, I will know exactly which of my ministers deserves his job and I can make sure I am not surrounded by stupid people."

The thieves looked at each other and smiled. "The magic material is very expensive to make," said one thief. "I'm not sure your excellency can afford it," said the other.

"Nonsense!" shouted the emperor. "Here, take a thousand gold coins, that should be more than enough to make the suit."

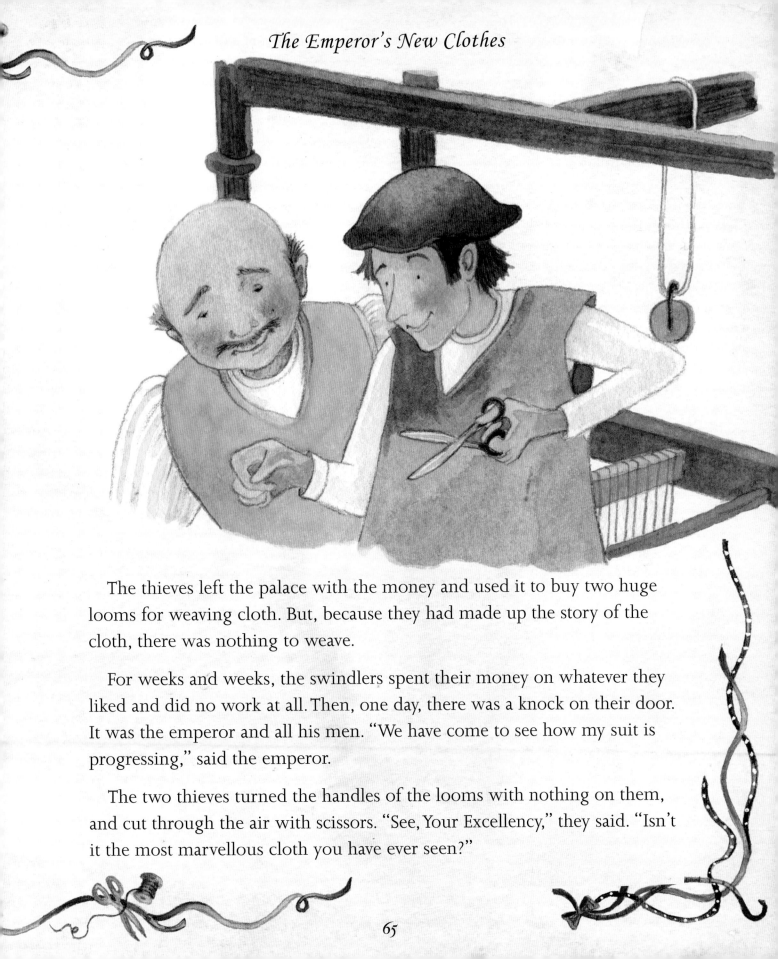

The thieves left the palace with the money and used it to buy two huge looms for weaving cloth. But, because they had made up the story of the cloth, there was nothing to weave.

For weeks and weeks, the swindlers spent their money on whatever they liked and did no work at all. Then, one day, there was a knock on their door. It was the emperor and all his men. "We have come to see how my suit is progressing," said the emperor.

The two thieves turned the handles of the looms with nothing on them, and cut through the air with scissors. "See, Your Excellency," they said. "Isn't it the most marvellous cloth you have ever seen?"

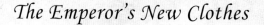

The emperor was shocked. He couldn't see any cloth at all. "Oh, no!" he thought. "It's just as I always thought. I'm either too stupid to see the cloth, or I don't deserve to be emperor. Nobody must ever know, or they would never let me rule." So he said to the thieves, "Yes, of course, it's certainly the finest cloth I have ever seen."

The thieves showed the imaginary cloth to the emperor's court, too. Each of them thought the same thing, "I must be too stupid, or unworthy, to see the cloth. I will pretend I can see it, so that the emperor does not punish me."

All the emperor's men pointed and applauded and said how fine the cloth was. "Of course, we'll need another thousand gold coins to finish it off," said the thieves. "After all, you wouldn't want to go outside with it half-finished like this." So, the emperor gave them the money without delay.

Many more weeks passed and the thieves returned to the palace. "We have finished the suit of clothes for you, Your Excellency," they said. They took the emperor into his rooms and pretended to fit the clothes on top of his under garments. "The cloth is so very fine and light, that only those with the most delicate skin can feel it," the thieves said. The emperor couldn't feel anything, of course, but he didn't want to look coarse and rough. "Oh, yes," he said. "It feels lighter than air."

When they were done, the thieves stood back and looked at the emperor, who was wearing nothing at all. "Our finest work!" the thieves said. "You are a marvel of modern fashion."

The emperor summoned his courtiers and they walked through the streets of the city. Everyone had heard of the magic cloth. To make sure nobody thought they were stupid, they all pretended that they could see the emperor's new clothes.

The procession wound its way through every street, even the very poorest ones. As they were passing one tiny house, a little girl and her father came out to watch them go past. The child hadn't heard about the magic cloth. "Look, Daddy," she said, "that funny man has come out in his underwear."

The child's father saw that his daughter was right. "You speak the truth, my dear," he said, laughing. "The emperor has no new clothes!"

The family next door heard the man and knew that what he said was true. "The emperor has no new clothes," they shouted. The message passed quickly from door to door and from street to street, until everyone in the city was pointing and laughing at the emperor. "The emperor has no new clothes!" they cried.

Finally, the emperor understood that what everyone was saying was true. At first, he was so embarrassed, he couldn't speak. But then, he too began to laugh, until he thought his sides would split. "I have been a proud and foolish man," he said to everyone, "and I have learned my lesson."

The thieves had fled the city and were never seen there again, but the emperor became a good and wise ruler who cared more about his people than his pride. And so the emperor and his people lived happily ever after.

# Snow White & Rose Red

Once upon a time, a poor widow lived with her two daughters. The girls were called Snow White and Rose Red. They were named after two rose trees that grew in front of their cottage – one red, and one white. They were very sweet and kind girls.

The two girls were very happy. When they weren't busy helping their mother, they played in the forest. The animals watched over them and always made sure they were safe. If they ever got lost, a kind bird or deer would lead them back to their cottage. On warm summer nights, they sometimes slept outside, beneath the moon. On cold winter nights, they warmed themselves beside the fire.

One cold winter's evening, they were sitting beside the fire when there was a knock at the door. Rose Red ran to pull it open.
"Aaaaahhhh!" she screamed. She was face to face with a big brown bear.
"Do not be afraid. I won't hurt you," said the bear in a surprisingly gentle voice. "May I come in to warm myself beside your fire?"
"Please do, you poor bear!" said the widow.

# Snow White & Rose Red

And she welcomed him in.

At first, Snow White and Rose Red were afraid of the big brown bear. Then, bit by bit, they became used to him. Before long, they were playing with him and having lots of fun.

For the rest of the winter, the bear was like one of the family. He slept beside the fire each night, and returned to the forest each day.

# Snow White & Rose Red

When spring arrived, the bear told the girls he had to go away. "I must guard my treasure from the wicked dwarfs who come out of their holes in the spring," he explained.

Later that day, Snow White and Rose Red were collecting firewood when they saw something dancing around a fallen tree. It was a angry-looking dwarf with a long, snow-white beard. His beard was trapped beneath the tree.
"What are you staring at?" he yelled at the girls. "Why don't you help?"

The girls pulled and pulled, but they could not free the beard.
"You useless brats," snarled the dwarf. "You're about as helpful as hole in the head. I could die before you get me out of here!"
"Don't worry," said Snow White. "I will help you."

Then she pulled her scissors out of her pocket and snipped his beard.
As soon as the dwarf was free, he grabbed a bag of gold from among the tree's roots and turned his back on the girls.
"Nasty girl, cutting off my fine beard," he hissed. And then he was gone.

Shortly afterwards, Snow White and Rose Red were walking by the brook when they saw the dwarf again. A big fish had caught hold of his beard and was pulling him into the water. The two girls caught hold of the dwarf and tried to pull him free. But it was no use. The fish was just too strong. Not knowing what else to do, Snow White pulled out her scissors and cut the beard.

"You toadstool!" screamed the dwarf once he was free. "Do you want to ruin all of my beautiful beard?" Then, without another word, he dragged a sack of pearls out of the reeds and disappeared.

A few days later, Snow White and Rose Red were walking to town when they heard someone scream. They ran towards the noise and saw that a huge eagle had grabbed the bad-tempered dwarf.
"Quick," said Rose Red. And each girl grabbed one of the dwarf's legs. They pulled and pulled until the eagle finally let go.

## Snow White & Rose Red

The dwarf jumped to his feet and grabbed a bag of jewels. "You clumsy creatures!" he snarled. "Couldn't you have been more careful? Look, my lovely coat is all torn." He glared at the girls with fiery red eyes, and then disappeared down a hole.

By now the girls were so used to the ungrateful dwarf's bad manners that they continued to town without giving him a further thought.

Later that evening, the girls were returning home when they saw something sparkling in the moonlight. The dwarf was pulling sacks of treasure out of a hole and spreading it out on the grass. It looked so lovely that the girls stopped to stare.

"What are you staring at?" screamed the dwarf in a rage.

He didn't stop shouting at them until there was a loud growl and a brown bear leaped out of the forest.

The dwarf was so scared that he didn't move an inch.

"D...d...dear Mr. Bear," he spluttered. "Don't hurt me. I'm just a skinny little dwarf. I wouldn't make much of a meal. Eat those girls instead. They are plump and juicy."

The bear paid no attention to his words. He sprung forward and cuffed the dwarf with a powerful paw. The dwarf gave a yell and fell to the ground.

Meanwhile, the two girls had run away to hide.

"Come back, Snow White and Rose Red," called the bear in a gentle voice.

"Don't be afraid. I won't hurt you."

It was their old friend, the bear.

Snow White and Rose Red ran to hug him. And when they did, the most surprising thing happened. His bearskin fell away to reveal a handsome young man, dressed from head to foot in gold.

"I am Prince Levi," he said. "That wicked dwarf stole my treasure and turned me into a bear. I was doomed to live as a bear for as long as he lived."

As Snow White gazed into the prince's sea-blue eyes, her heart began to pound. She was falling in love. Luckily, Prince Levi felt exactly the same.

## Snow White & Rose Red

Not long afterwards, there was a huge wedding. Snow White married Prince Levi and Rose Red married his brother, Prince Sebastian. The girls and their mother moved to the castle, and they all shared the treasure. But none of the treasure was as dear to them as the two rose trees that grew outside the castle gates – one red and one white.

# Cinderella

Once upon a time, there was a man who had a beautiful wife and a lovely daughter, called Ella. When his wife died, the man married another woman, who had two daughters of her own. They became Ella's step-sisters, but they were jealous of her and treated her like a servant. Poor Ella had to wear old, tatty clothes and do all the housework.

One day, Ella was in the kitchen, cleaning out the grate, when the two step-sisters came to see her. Ella's ragged clothes were stained and her face was covered in soot. "Look how dirty she is," crowed one sister, fluttering her fan. "She's covered with ashes and cinders."

"We should call her Cinder-Ella!" said the other sister.

From that moment on, Ella became known as Cinderella.

One day, news arrived at the house that the prince of the land was going to hold a Grand Ball at the palace. Cinderella's father made sure that his new wife, as well as Cinderella and her two step-sisters, were invited, but when the invitations came, the sisters tore up Cinderella's before she saw it. "Too bad," they said, "the prince doesn't want you in his beautiful palace."

When the night of the ball came, Cinderella had to help her stepmother and her stepsisters dress in their fancy gowns. Then she was sent back to the kitchen, to do all the washing, while they left for the ball. When all the work was done, Cinderella sat in the cold kitchen and cried. "I'm so sad and lonely," she said, "won't anyone help me?"

The chimney of the big kitchen fireplace began to glow and sparkle, then something bright rushed out. A sparking, fizzing light circled the kitchen and a kind-looking fairy appeared, in a shower of sparks.
"Who are you?" asked Cinderella, in surprise.
"I'm your Fairy Godmother," answered the fairy, "and you look in need of help. What can I do for you?"

Cinderella explained that she wasn't allowed to go to the Grand Ball.
"Don't worry," said the Fairy Godmother, "you shall go to the ball!"
"But how can I go dressed in these rags?" asked Cinderella.
"A little magic will fix that," said the fairy godmother, sweetly." She waved her wand around Cinderella's head and her rags fluttered and flapped and swished and swelled, until they had turned into the most amazing ballgown Cinderella had ever seen. It even had a pair of glass slippers to match.

"Of course, you'll need to get to the ball," added the Fairy Godmother. She waved her wand over a pumpkin and it became a magnificent, sparkly, gold coach. Cinderella was amazed and thrilled to see the wonderful coach.

Next, the Fairy Godmother searched around the garden and found a lizard and four mice. She waved her wand over them and they were transformed into a coachman and four beautiful horses. "Now you can go to the ball," said the Fairy Godmother. "But remember, all my magic stops at midnight. So make sure that you are back here before then."

When Cinderella entered the ball at the palace, all eyes were upon her.
The handsome prince took one look at her and fell instantly in love.
He spent every minute of the night dancing with her.

Cinderella enjoyed herself so much, she forgot to watch the big clock that
hung at one end of the ballroom. "I am falling in love with you," the prince
told Cinderella, as they danced. "Do you love me because of my fine
clothes?" asked Cinderella.
"I would love you, even if you were in rags," said the prince.

Suddenly, the clock began to strike midnight. Terrified of showing herself in her dirty rags, Cinderella broke free of the prince and ran out of the palace. In her haste, she left behind one of her glass slippers. As she was running down the palace steps, the gown turned back into rags, the coach became a pumpkin again and the rats and lizard scuttled away. Cinderella ran back to her house and nobody knew that she had ever left it.

The prince swore that he would find the owner of the slipper. "The girl whose foot fits this slipper is the girl I shall marry," he said. The prince and his pages visited every house in the land and every girl, in every house, tried on the slipper. But it was so small and dainty, nobody's foot would fit into it.

At last, the prince came to Cinderella's house. "He mustn't see you," her stepmother said, so the sisters locked Cinderella in the coal cellar and was hidden from the prince. The two sisters both tried to make the shoe fit but, no matter how hard they squeezed, they couldn't squash their big feet into the tiny, delicate, glass slipper.

The prince was ready to leave when he heard knocking coming from the cellar door. Opening it, he was surprised to see a young girl dressed in rags and covered in ash and coal dust. "Let this girl try on the slipper," said the prince.

Cinderella tried the slipper on and her little foot slipped into it perfectly. The prince knew immediately that Cinderella was the girl he had danced with at the palace.

"Will you marry me and be my queen?" asked the prince. Cinderella had never felt so happy and accepted joyfully. The prince banished the wicked stepmother and the stepsisters to a faraway land and Cinderella and the prince were married without delay. Cinderella's father came to live with them in the Prince's palace and all three of them lived happily ever after.

# The Robot Nan

Every Wednesday, Olive and Erica's Nan picked them up from school. This particular Wednesday, Erica's teacher Mrs. Williams brought Erica out, her face spotted with orange and blue paint.

"I'm sorry Erica is late," said Mrs. Williams. "She wanted to finish what she was doing."

"And what was that?" laughed Nan. "Having a paint fight?"

"Certainly not," sighed Erica. "I was inventing a flying machine. But I just can't get it to work."

## The Robot Nan

Olive was waiting on a bench in the playground, kicking her legs angrily. "You're always late," she grouched.

"Inventing a flying machine takes time," grinned Erica.

"Why bother with a flying machine?" said Olive, watching her Nan walk slowly towards them. "Why not invent something more useful?"

Nan lived in a ground-floor apartment across town. Olive slipped her arm through her Nan's to walk the short distance from the bus stop. Erica ran ahead, hiding behind lamp posts. "Chase me, Nan!" she puffed.

"Ssh!" whispered Olive, elbowing her younger sister. "Nan can't run."

Nan peered into her big, silver handbag, looking for keys. "I want to run," she said, "and climb trees. But when I was around your age, Erica, my bones and joints started misbehaving. Sometimes it's difficult to move around."

"If your bones aren't behaving," frowned Erica, "you should put them on 'time out.'" Nan chuckled. "They were on 'time out' for a long time," she said. "They didn't trouble me for years. But now they've started being mis-behaving again . . . Olive, could you please unlock the door for me?"

## The Robot Nan

Inside, the girls flung off their shoes and ran straight to the kitchen. Olive filled the kettle and Erica stood on a stool to retrieve a tin marked "Cake"
"Brownies," said Erica, looking inside. "Yummy."

The doors between the living room and garden were open. Herby scents wafted in. Nan was sitting outside, waiting. "Tea, cake… what's missing?" she smiled.

Erica scurried out. She returned clutching an old-fashioned spinning top. Faded pictures and scratches suggested the toy had been well-used.
"Whose turn is it?" teased Nan.
"Mine!" Olive grabbed the top from Erica's hands and pumped the handle. Painted figures danced in a circle, quicker and quicker until the patterns merged into a pale silver stream.
"It's humming!" Erica yelled excitedly. "Come on, Nan."
"Ready?" The girls nodded eagerly. Nan started. "I have a spinning top that . . ." ". . . takes me back in time," the girls joined in.

Every Wednesday, they spun the top and Nan told a story about her Caribbean childhood. It was funny imagining their grandmother as a naughty girl chasing chickens or catching tadpoles in the bamboo-fringed streams. But this Wednesday Nan surprised them.
"I have a spinning top that . . . takes me forward in time," she said.
Erica and Olive looked at each other.
"A long, long way forward, when I'm a robot nan with hands of steel and arms that ping in and out. I can walk forever and jump so high that my eyebrows reach the clouds."
"Robots don't have eyebrows," said Olive uncertainly. "This one does," said Nan. "And she has two brave assistants called Erica and Olive."

The girls' father came for them at seven o'clock. "What was the story today?" he asked, as they drove across town. "Did she chase the enormous black toad from the porch? Or was it when the anaconda fell on Granddad's head?" "She was a robot," said Olive. "With super-strong arms and legs."

"But that's not true," said Erica. 'cause her fingers hurt so much today that Olive had to unlock the front door."

For the next two days, Erica's room was full of crumpled drawings and she refused to explain what they were. Olive grew impatient. "Forget about your silly flying machine!" But Erica just smiled mysteriously.

Olive finally banged on her door, she was desperate to know what Erica was up to. "Erica, please let me in," she begged. The bedroom door opened a sliver. A long piece of paper fluttered from Erica's fingers. "If you want to help with my invention, this is what I need!"

Olive looked at the list and sighed. It took all morning and much pleading with her parents to find everything, "why do you need Dad's luggage wheels?" she complained. "And a mop or old bicycle clips? I had to open my birthday science kit to get you a magnet, so I definitely want that back. Sewing stuff, plastic gloves. Dad's gone out for plaster of Paris and says there are no old sheets, but you can have this curtain. This is 'going to be the weirdest flying machine ever!" "It's not a flying machine," beamed Erica. "Look!"

Olive looked. "Wow!" she said, and followed Erica into the bedroom.

# The Robot Nan

Nan came for lunch on Sunday. The girls busied themselves with the final details of Erica's invention.

"Ready?" their mother was outside the bedroom. The door opened. Erica wore one of Dad's old white shirts, like a scientist's coat. Olive held a clipboard and pen. Their mother stared into the room. "I'd better help you carry it downstairs!" she laughed.

Nan was sitting with Dad at the garden table.

"So the world's two best inventors have been at work all weekend!" she said. Erica ran up and hugged her. "Yes, and we've made something especially for you!"

Their mother placed the covered object carefully on the ground. Erica whipped off the blanket. Olive's old school backpack was tied to luggage wheels and decorated with pom-poms.

"A wheely bag!" said Nan. "Wonderful!"

"That's just the carrying case," Olive explained. "Look inside!"

Nan reached in and pulled out the mop pole. A bicycle clip was tied to the end instead of the mop head. Nan pushed the button on the handle that made the pole longer. She chuckled. Then she laughed and wiped her eyes. Erica and Olive looked at each other uncertainly.

"Do you know what it is, Nan?" asked Olive

"Of course." Nan waved the pole in the air. "It's my robot arm!"

"Yes," said Erica excitedly. "The bicycle clip can hold a can while you open it." Olive delved into the backpack-on-wheels.

"We made the arm so you can add on different things." She laid a bright red magnet on the table. "This is to find pins or paperclips."

Nan picked up a plaster of Paris hand that had a pointing forefinger.

The girls had glued ribbons on it so that it could be tied around the pole.

# The Robot Nan

"You can poke people if they're far away," Erica explained. "And make holes in your garden for worms. I made it by pouring plaster of Paris into a rubber glove."

Nan tied the hand to the pole. "Now I really am a Robot Nan!" she said. She pushed the button on the stick so the end flew out and the plaster finger poked Dad's shoulder.

"Robot pointy-thing alert!" he laughed.

Nan put an arm around the girls' shoulders and gathered them in for a hug. "Ready for another Robot Nan story?" she asked.

"Well . . ." said Erica.

"We would rather hear about when you were little," finished Olive.

Nan lay the robot arm on the table and slowly straightened her fingers. "Have I told you about the spider as big as a bird?" she asked.

"No," squealed the girls. "Tell us!"

# The Magic Music Box

Annabel wanted nothing more than to be able to dance. Her grandmother had been a very famous dancer, and Annabel would spend hours looking at all the old photographs and trophies at her grandparents' house. She would imagine herself on stage, in the spotlight, doing ballet in front of a huge crowd.

But no matter how hard she tried, Annabel couldn't make her feet do what she wanted them to. She watched enviously as the other girls in her ballet class twirled across the floor. "Why am I so clumsy?" she would sigh.

One day, Annabel was visiting her grandparents' house, when her grandma took her aside. "How are the dancing lessons going, Annabel?" she asked.
"Oh Nana, I just can't do it!" cried Annabel. "I'm always practicing, but I just can't get it right."
"Of course you can!" laughed her grandmother. "You just have to believe you can do it. Now wait there a moment. I have something for you."

Nana came back with a cardboard box and handed it to Annabel.
"Well, open it!" she laughed.

Inside the box, hidden beneath crumpled brown paper, was the prettiest, most delicate music box Annabel had ever seen. She opened it to find a little fairy ballerina spinning around to a simple, elegant melody.
"It's beautiful Nana! Thank you!" cried Annabel.

# The Magic Music Box

"It belonged to me when I was a little girl," said Nana. "You must promise to take very good care of it. This music box is magical. It will make you the most fantastic ballet dancer!"

Annabel was thrilled to be given such a wonderful gift. She gave her Nana a big hug and then ran off to show her parents.

## The Magic Music Box

A week later, Annabel had an audition for a big part in her part in her ballet school's end of year show. Since her Nana had given her the magical music box, Annabel had been feeling very brave. She knew that she would be able to dance wonderfully in the show, as long as she had magic on her side.

She walked out onto the stage and the music began. From then on the audition was a blur of spinning, jumping and swirling light and sound. Annabel was lost in the music and dancing.

When her audition was over, Annabel was in in a daze. She got changed and went to meet her parents and grandparents. They all told her how amazing she had been. The music box had worked its magic!

"I've never seen you dance better, Annabel," said Nana, giving her a hug. "I'm so proud of you." Then she took her hand and whispered in her ear, "The music box isn't magic, Annabel. You were a wonderful dancer all along. You just had to have some confidence in yourself."

Annabel could only stare in amazement as her grandmother laughed and gave her a huge hug. She had become a wonderful ballet dancer at last.

# Treasure Island

Zoe and Amy lived with their mother and father and a puppy called Jake in a white cottage overlooking the sea, with a path of crushed shells that ran down to a rocky beach below.

The two girls loved swimming, and spent almost all their spare time on the beach, or in the water. They practically lived in their bathing suits or wetsuits, and had earned themselves the name of 'The Water Babes' in their family.

One sunny afternoon, Zoe and Amy were having a picnic in the garden with their mother, looking out over the sea as they ate.

Suddenly, Zoe spoke. "Have you ever been to that island, Mum?" she asked, pointing to a small mound rising up out of the water off the shore.

"Oh yes," replied Mum. "But it was a very long time ago. It has a beautiful white sandy beach on the other side, where seals bask in the sunshine."

Their mother closed her eyes for a moment, as if remembering.
Then she smiled a long slow smile. "And do you know why I was there?" she asked. "For treasure!"

"You mean there's treasure on the island?" asked Amy excitedly.
"Yes," laughed their mother. "Buried by a big white rock."

All afternoon, the girls could talk of nothing but treasure, and how to get to the island. They were still talking about it at bedtime that night.

"It's too far to swim," said Zoe, as she climbed into bed and snuggled under the covers. "I guess we'll never get to see it."

# Treasure Island

The next morning, the girls woke up early. Zoe looked out of the window and gasped. "Look!" she cried to Amy. There on the beach were their mother and father ... and a little red wooden rowing boat. Zoe and Amy had never moved so fast! Wetsuits and life jackets pulled on, they raced down to the shore. "Girls, meet Rosie the rowing boat" said Dad proudly. "She's ready for her first adventure."

The girls climbed eagerly into the little boat, then Dad launched it into the water, and jumped aboard. They were off to their treasure island.

Just a few minutes later, Dad was pulling the little boat up onto the shore of the island. "We need to find a big white rock," Amy said.
"I see it, I see it," shouted Zoe, running over to a large white boulder glinting in the sun. "Quick! Help me turn it over."

The rock was very heavy, but between them they rolled it away. Underneath they found a battered wooden box with a rusty catch. Zoe found a stick and jammed it under the catch. Finally, the lock sprang open.
"Wow!" the girls cried in unison. "It really is treasure!"
Inside was a gold locket, a ruby ring, a purse of coins and some photographs of their Mum when she was a little girl.

When they got back to the beach at home, their Mum was waiting for them. "I see you've found my treasure," she laughed. "I put that box there many years ago, when I was about your age. And since you found it, it's only right that you should keep it."

"Thank you!" cried Zoe and Amy, hugging their mother tightly.
"And now we must make our own treasure chest and bury it on the island. Then someone else can find it one day."

# The Magic Cake

Once there was a young princess who was greatly loved by all the servants in her palace. Although she was happy to spend time with her royal parents, the princess enjoyed sneaking away to visit the palace kitchens.

The chief cook was the princess' special friend. She was a big, round woman with twinkling eyes. Her hands were dusty with flour and her cheeks were always rosy red. The cook was cheerful most of the time, except when the greedy palace cats tried to steal food from her kitchen table. Then the cook would wave her rolling pin and chase them away.

Each day, the princess helped the cook make pies and pastries and sometimes she was allowed to lick the sticky spoon when the cook was making her famous cakes.

The princess' birthday was approaching, so she decided to invite all her friends to a big party to celebrate. It was going to be the social event of the season and the princess couldn't wait to eat her birthday cake.

# The Magic Cake

One night, just before her birthday, the princess ran down the stairs to the big kitchen. But, when she opened the door, the princess got a surprise. The cook was waving her rolling pin like a magic wand. Around her, all the pots, pans and cutlery were jumping into the kitchen sink to clean themselves. Then they dried themselves and flew into the kitchen cupboards.

When the cook saw the princess, she made all the magic disappear with a wave of her rolling pin wand. "I'm an enchantress," explained the cook, "but, if people saw me use my powers, they might think I was a witch. So I only use them to clean the kitchen. If you agree to keep my secret, I will make you an extra-special birthday cake."

The princess agreed to keep the cook's secret. She would never have told on her friend, anyway. Still, she was very excited that she was going to get a special birthday cake.

The princess told all her friends about the extra-special cake. But, when her birthday arrived and all the guests went to sit at the table, the princess was disappointed to see a simple cake with nothing more than white icing and a few candles in the middle.

"How dull!" said some of the guests to each other and laughed. The princess wished she hadn't said anything to her friends. She cut the cake anyway and gave a slice to each of the guests.

As the princess was cutting a piece of cake for herself, she noticed a slip of paper stuck to the icing. It had a message from the cook which said, "More cake changes you back." The princess was very puzzled, but she took a big bite of the delicious cake and thought about what the note might mean.

Suddenly, the princess felt a tickle on her shoulders. Looking round, she saw that she had sprouted bright, feathery rainbow wings. When she looked around the table, she saw that all her guests were growing wings, too.

Next, the party guests began to shrink and became the size of fairies. Everyone squealed with excitement, as they realised they could fly.

"I knew the cake would be magic!" said the princess and she led her guests out into the palace corridors. They giggled and shrieked with delight, as they flew into every room, swooping and diving. They were like excited fairies, flitting here, there and everywhere.

After lots of zooming around the huge palace, the party guests began to feel tired. Flying was fun, but it was very hard work. "We can't keep our wings, forever," they said. "But how do we change back?"

The princess remembered the note from the cook. Now she understood what it meant. "We have to eat more cake," said the princess.

So, with a great fluttering of their rainbow wings, everyone flew back to the cake on the table. But the greedy palace cats had got there first. They were eating the cake and hissed at anyone who tried to stop them.

"If we don't eat more cake," said the princess, "we'll have to stay this size forever!" The princess swooped down towards the table. The cats swiped at her with their sharp claws, but she was too fast for them and grabbed a huge piece of cake.

As soon as the princess and the guests had eaten the cake, they lost their wings and grew to their full size again. Everyone was exhausted, but happy. "The was the best party ever!" said the guests.

The princess thanked the cook for her special cake. The cook promised that, at least once a year, on her birthday, the princess would always have some magic cake, so that she and her friends could fly like real fairies.

# The Snow Queen

Once upon a time, there was a boy named Kay and a girl named Gerda. They were best friends and loved to play together among the flowers in Gerda's garden.

One winter's day, when they were playing outside in the snow, Kay tasted a snowflake that was falling from the sky. The snowflake was cursed by dark magic and suddenly, Kay felt his heart grow cold. Instead of seeing the goodness in all that was around him, he only noticed the things that were bad and ugly.

From that day on, Kay didn't play with Gerda. Instead, he preferred to look at snowflakes with his magnifying glass. "Snowflakes are much nicer than flowers," said Kay. "Flowers are boring!"

Poor Gerda was left alone, while Kay played on his sled with all the older boys. One day, a strange, white sleigh stopped nearby. It was pulled by two beautiful, white horses and Kay tied his sled to it. To his surprise, the sleigh sped off across the snow and pulled him along for many miles.

When it stopped, Kay saw a pale lady, dressed in white fur.
"I am the Snow Queen," she said. Come under my cloak to get warm."
So Kay slipped under the cloak of the Snow Queen. As he did, his heart
froze over. He forgot all about Gerda and the friends he had left behind.

The Snow Queen took Kay by the hand and they flew through the air.
They landed in the frozen north, at the Snow Queen's ice palace, which had
a great lake at the centre. The palace was a mighty fortress of snow and ice
and the Snow Queen made Kay a prisoner there. He had no memory of
Gerda, or his old life.

"I must go on a long journey," said the Snow Queen. "By the time I get
back, I want you to put all the ice on my lake back together." The ice on the
Snow Queen's lake had split into hundreds of pieces, like a giant jigsaw
puzzle. Kay sat by the frozen lake and moved the pieces around, but the
puzzle was impossible to solve.

Meanwhile, Gerda spent her days looking everywhere for Kay. She spoke to the older boys, who told Gerda that Kay had gone north with a strange sleigh. So she walked and walked, through fields and forests. Wherever Gerda went, she asked about Kay, but nobody had seen him.

After many adventures, Gerda found herself in a cold land. There was nobody to be seen, except for a herd of reindeer. As they trotted past, she called out to them, "Have you seen my friend, Kay?"

The reindeer walked past, as if they hadn't heard her, except for one old reindeer. "I have seen this boy," he said. "He was being carried on a sleigh with the Snow Queen. She traps boys and keeps them in her ice palace."

When she heard this, Gerda wept. "I'll never find Kay," she said. "Don't worry," replied the reindeer. "The palace is far to the north. I can travel very fast through snow and ice, so I will take you there."

Gerda climbed onto the reindeer's warm and furry back, then they galloped far to the north. At first, there were thick forests on the hills around them but soon, the grass disappeared and the trees died away. After a while, they were surrounded by snow and ice.

Gerda and the reindeer travelled for countless days, until it was so cold that Gerda could barely move. Ahead of them, the night sky was filled with the shimmering, glowing rainbow bands of the northern lights, that lit the reindeer's way.

Finally, Gerda and the reindeer reached the North Pole. They found a great palace that looked as if it had been carved from a single block of ice. "This must be the ice palace," said Gerda.

As Gerda approached, there was a strange, low, rumbling noise. The sound grew louder and then, suddenly, ice creatures, shaped like great bears, rose up from the snow and stood guard at the entrance to the palace. Gerda was afraid, but she found that her hot breath melted the creatures and she passed safely through the entrance to the palace.

Inside, the ice palace was vast and silent. Gerda marvelled at the huge, freezing halls, whose ceilings seemed to stretch upwards to the sky. She shivered in the cold. "I must find Kay," whispered Gerda and she continued to search the Snow Queen's palace.

There were giant, empty halls everywhere. Gerda walked through them and found Kay sitting by the lake, moving pieces of ice around in a daze.

Gerda ran to Kay. She hugged him, but he didn't even notice her. He was too busy trying to solve the impossible puzzle the Snow Queen had set him. Gerda began to cry and her tears touched Kay's face. The warm tears melted all the ice around Kay's heart. He sat up and looked around, as if waking from a dream. "Oh Gerda!" he said, "I'm so glad you're here."

The two friends ran from the frozen palace. Its vast halls echoed with their footsteps. Outside, they climbed onto the reindeer's back and galloped off, before the Snow Queen could return.

It was a long and tiring journey. After many days, the weary friends arrived home, to find that it was summer and the flowers were in bloom. Kay and Gerda played together in the garden, just as they used to do and never again did the Snow Queen freeze Kay's heart.

# Goldilocks and the Three Bears

Once upon a time, there were three bears who lived in a cottage in the woods. There was Father Bear, Mother Bear and Baby Bear. One day, Mother Bear made porridge for breakfast, but it was too hot to eat, so the bears decided to go for a walk until it cooled down.

Meanwhile, a little girl called Goldilocks was walking in the woods.
It wasn't long before Goldilocks realised that she was lost. She wandered
through the forest, trying to find her way home, but soon she became cold
and hungry.

Goldilocks was feeling very fed up when she came upon the three bears'
cottage. "Maybe someone lives here who can help me," she said. She went
up to the little cottage and knocked on the door, but nobody answered.
Goldilocks peered into a window, but she couldn't see anybody inside.
So she tried the door and found it was open.

Goldilocks stepped inside the cottage. "Is anybody home?" she asked, but there was no reply because the three bears were still out on their morning walk. Goldilocks went to the kitchen and saw three bowls of porridge on the table. "I'm so hungry, I'm sure nobody will mind if I just have a taste," she thought to herself.

Goldilocks tasted the biggest bowl of porridge, but it was too hot.

So she tasted the middle bowl of porridge, but it was too cold.

Then Goldilocks tasted the smallest bowl of porridge and it was just right. So she gobbled it all up.

When Goldilocks had finished the porridge, her tummy felt really full. "I think I will find somewhere comfortable to sit down and have a rest," she said.

Goldilocks looked around and saw three chairs. The first chair was very big and Goldilocks found it hard to climb up onto the seat.

So, she tried the middle chair instead. It was a bit better, but it was still too high.

However, when Goldilocks tried the smallest chair, it seemed to be just right

Goldilocks sat back on the chair and was just getting comfortable when suddenly, the legs snapped and she fell to the floor.

"I'm sleepy," thought Goldilocks, so she went upstairs and found a bedroom with three beds in it. There was a big one, a medium-sized one, and a tiny little one.

Goldilocks jumped onto the biggest bed, but it was far too hard.

So, she tried sleeping on the middle-sized bed, but it was far too soft.

Goldilocks laid down on the smallest bed. It was just right, so she laid her head on the pillow and fell fast asleep.

Soon, the three bears finished their walk and returned to the cottage. They were surprised to see that the front door was open. They went into the kitchen and Father Bear looked at the big bowl. "Someone's been eating my porridge," he said.

Mother Bear looked at the middle bowl, which had a spoon sticking out of it. "Someone's been eating my porridge," she said.

Baby Bear looked at the small bowl. "Someone's been eating MY porridge," he said, "and they've eaten it all up!"

Father Bear went to sit down, but the big chair wasn't in its usual place. "Someone's been sitting in my chair," he said.

Mother Bear saw that the middle chair had been moved, too. "Someone's been sitting in my chair," she said.

Baby Bear looked at the small chair lying smashed on the floor. "Someone's been sitting in MY chair," he wailed, "and they've broken it to pieces!" Baby Bear started to cry.

The three bears went upstairs to their bedroom. Father Bear saw that the sheets had fallen off the biggest bed. "Someone's been sleeping in my bed," he said.

Mother Bear looked at the crumpled pillows on the medium-sized bed. "Someone's been sleeping in my bed," she said.

Baby Bear pointed at the smallest bed. "Someone's been sleeping in MY bed," he said, "and she's still there!"

Suddenly, Goldilocks woke up with a start. She sat up and saw the three bears looking down at her. With a shriek, she scrambled out of the bed, ran downstairs and out of the cottage, into the woods. She didn't dare look behind her, in case the three bears were following her. But the three bears were still in the bedroom, scratching their heads and wondering why a little golden-haired girl had gone to sleep in Baby Bear's bed.

Goldilocks ran so fast, she soon found herself back home again. She rushed in and hugged her mother who had been worrying where she was. After that, Goldilocks didn't go into the woods by herself and she never went back to the Three bears' cottage again.

# The Six Swans

Once upon a time, there lived a King who had one daughter and six sons. The King loved his children very much, for his wife had died many years earlier and they were the only relations he had left in the world.

One day, the King went hunting. He rode deeper and deeper into the woods following a stag, until all at once he realized he was lost. Each way he turned the paths looked the same. He grew more and more worried until suddenly he spotted an old woman sitting on a tree trunk.
"Excuse me," said the King politely. "Could you show me the way out of the woods so I can find my way home?"

The woman saw his royal robes and realized at once that he was a King.
"I will show you on one condition," she answered slyly. "You must marry my beautiful daughter and take her to be Queen of your land."
"And what if I do not care to take the hand of your daughter?"
asked the King.
"Then I will leave you alone for the wild animals to hunt!" she replied.

The King was worried about his children, so he was forced to agree.

The next day the King kept his word and married the woman's daughter. But he saw that she would not be a kind stepmother to his children, so he asked his servants to hide his family in a castle, deep in the oak forest.

Every morning, before the sun rose, the King left his wife sleeping and went to visit his children. Then he crept back to his bed before his wife noticed. One day, however, his wife woke early and noticed that he was gone. The same thing happened the next morning. She became suspicious and decided to follow him.

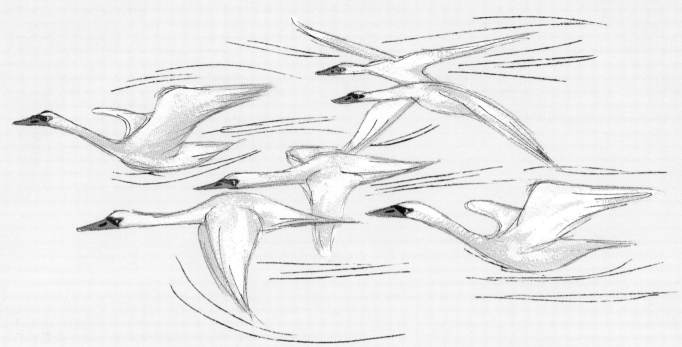

On seeing that he had seven children hiding in a castle, the Queen became very angry. She took a ball of magic string she had been given by her mother and, using a spell she had learned from her, turned the string into magic shirts made of pure white silk.

The next time the King went out hunting, the evil Queen hurried to the castle in the oak forest. Thinking it was their father arriving, the six boys rushed outside to greet him. Immediately, the Queen threw the magic shirts over them. At once, the six boys were turned into six white swans, and all flew away.

When the King went to visit his children the next morning, only his daughter remained. He was heartbroken when she told him what had happened.
"You must stay here until I can find a new, safe place to hide you," he told her.

That night, as the winds howled, the daughter was sure she heard her brothers calling in the forest, so she left the castle to look for them. All night she searched and searched, until she could go no further.

At last she spotted a hut. "Maybe I can shelter here," she thought, opening the door. Inside she saw six beds. She longed to lie down, but she was worried that the owners might return, so she hid herself under one and closed her eyes to sleep.

# The Six Swans

The girl was woken by the sound of beating wings. Opening her eyes, she was amazed to see six swans land on the beds. As each landed, its feathers fell off, revealing her six handsome young brothers.

"My brothers!" she cried, climbing out from under the bed.

They were overjoyed to see each her, and they all hugged tightly. But the brothers were worried, too.

"You must not stay here," they told her. "This hut isn't safe. We cannot protect you, for we are only human for a few moments each day before we turn back into swans."

"There must be something I can do to help?" said their sister.

# The Six Swans

"There is," replied her oldest brother, "but it will not be easy. For six years you must not speak or laugh. And in your solitude you must sew six shirts made of the tiniest flower petals."

Before another word could be spoken, the six brothers turned back into swans and flew away. At once, their sister set off in search of the tiniest flowers she could find. Her search took her to another kingdom, where a carpet of the daintiest flowers she had ever seen grew on the forest floor. There she sat down and began to sew.

The next day the King of the land passed by.
"What are you sewing with my prettiest flowers?" he questioned. But the girl could not speak, of course, so she just kept on sewing.

The King was enchanted by this beautiful silent girl who sewed so diligently. He visited her every day, and every day he fell a little more in love with her. Before the summer was over, he had persuaded her to marry him, even though she had never spoken a word.

# The Six Swans

The King's mother did not like this new, silent girl. So she decided upon a plan to get rid of her. After the girl gave birth to the King's first child, the mother stole the baby and spread lies that the girl had given it away. The young Queen's heart was broken, but she could not speak to say what had happened, so she just carried on sewing. The King, who loved his wife, refused to believe the lies.

When the young Queen had another child and it too went missing, the evil mother demanded that her son take action. But the King still loved his wife dearly, and knew in his heart that she would never give away their child. When the third child went missing, however, the King began to doubt his heart. "My wife wants to do nothing more than sew all day long, every day," he thought. "Perhaps my mother is right about her."

"Surely, if your wife is not guilty then she would tell you so," said the evil mother. Of course, the young Queen could not speak the truth, or any other words, so the King mistrusted his heart and decided she should be punished.

The next day was the day of the Queen's judgment. But it was also the end of the Queen's six years of silence. All through the night she sewed and sewed.

By morning she had finished the six shirts, except for the last sleeve of one.

As the Queen stood before the King, her fate to be decided, the air was filled  with the noise of beating wings and the trumpeting of swans. At once, the Queen threw the petal shirts over the swans' heads and the spell was finally broken. Before her stood her six brothers, one with a wing of a swan as an arm, for it was that shirt she had not finished in time.

"At last I can speak!" she cried. When the King learned what his mother had done, he sent her away forever. The six brothers took it upon themselves to find their missing nieces and nephews the mother had hidden, and it was to great celebration that they returned home with the missing children. The King was so grateful he invited his wife's brothers to live with them, for their father had passed away in the six years gone.

And so it was that the King, Queen, their children and the six brothers all lived together in happiness for the rest of their lives.

# Rumpelstiltskin

Once upon a time, a king visited a humble miller. The miller longed to impress the king, so he boasted about his beautiful daughter. "My daughter is a very good spinner," said the miller. "She can spin straw into gold!"

The king was amazed to hear this. He ordered the miller's daughter to be locked in a tower in his castle. He left her there with a heap of straw and a spinning wheel. "You have three days to spin all this straw into gold," said the king. "If you fail, you will be punished."

But the poor miller's daughter couldn't really spin straw into gold. Her father had lied to the king and now she had been set an impossible task. The miller's daughter sat in the tower room and wept.

Suddenly, the stone wall of the tower seemed to ripple like water and a strange little man stepped through. He was short and had an ugly, bearded little face. "What's all this noise?" asked the man, grumpily. The miller's daughter explained her problem.

The little man stroked his hairy chin. "What will you give me if I spin this straw into gold?" he asked. The miller's daughter thought hard. "You can have my necklace," she said.

The man looked at the girl's necklace and nodded. He sat at the spinning wheel and began to spin. By morning, he had spun some of the straw into gold. Then, as quickly as he had arrived, the strange little man disappeared back into the wall.

The next morning, the king was pleased when he saw the gold, but he wanted more. "If the rest of the straw isn't spun into gold in two days, you will be punished," he said to the miller's daughter.

That night, the little man returned. "What will you give me if I spin you more gold?" he asked. The miller's daughter gave him her bracelet and the man spun more of the straw into gold.

When the king came to collect the gold the next morning, he was very happy. He thought the miller's daughter was beautiful and he almost told her to stop spinning, but he couldn't resist wanting more gold. "You must spin the remaining straw into gold tonight," he said.

That night, the miller's daughter waited and waited for the little man to appear. It was past midnight before the wall rippled and he stepped out. "Quick," she said. "You must spin the rest of the straw into gold, or I shall be in great trouble."

The little man grinned at her. "What will you give me if I do?" But the miller's daughter had nothing left to give to him.

"I will spin this straw into gold for you," said the man, "if you promise to give me your first-born child."

The miller's daughter was so frightened, she agreed. The little man sat at the wheel and worked faster than ever. Just as the sun came up, the last straw was spun into gold. The little man disappeared through the wall and the king opened the door.

The king was so amazed at the miller's daughter's skill and beauty that he asked her to marry him straight away. The miller's daughter agreed, as long as the king never asked her to spin gold into straw again.

The king was married to the miller's daughter and she became the queen. In time, she had a beautiful, baby daughter. She had forgotten all about her promise until one day, the wall of her room rippled like water and the strange little man stepped out. "You made a promise to give me your first-born child," he said.

The queen hugged her baby tight and would not let her go. "Take all my riches instead," she pleaded.

"No!" snapped the little man in triumph. "Only those who know my name have power over me. You do not know my name, so I will take your baby and you cannot stop me."

"Wait," said the queen, trying to think quickly. "It took you three days to spin the straw, so I should have three days to guess your name."

"Very well," said the little man. "But in three days, your baby is mine!"

The next day, when the man reappeared, the queen tried all the names she could think of. The little man just laughed and said, "no," to every one that she suggested.

On the second day, the queen searched through every book in the castle's great library. There was nothing about a little man who could spin straw into gold. Once again, the cackling man appeared and then disappeared when the queen failed to guess his name.

On the morning of the third day, the queen was in despair at not being able to figure out the man's name. She took her baby out with her and walked for miles, through fields and forests.

Just as the queen was ready to give up, she saw a thin line of smoke, floating through the trees. Following it, she saw a funny little house. Outside the house, there was a small fire. The little man who had spun gold from straw was dancing around the fire, laughing and singing a strange song.

The queen crouched down by the trees and kissed her baby to make sure she made no noise. Then she listened to the little man's song.
"The queen's daughter I'll surely claim.
The queen can't beat me at my game.
Rumplestiltskin is my name!"
The queen crept away and then rushed back to the castle, as fast as she could.

Later that night, just as he had done before, the strange little man appeared. "Your time is up," he said. The child is mine, so hand her over. I will take her to Fairyland and she will grow up to be my slave." The little man clapped his hands with glee.

"I have one last guess," said the queen. "I think that your name is Rumplestiltskin."

When Rumpelstiltskin heard his name being spoken, he was enraged. His face was red with fury. He jumped up and down and stamped so hard on the ground, he made a great hole in it. Then he disappeared through the wall, still shouting and screaming with rage. After that, Rumpelstiltskin was never seen, or heard of again.

The king and queen's daughter grew up to be a beautiful young woman. No one ever told her that she was once nearly spirited off to Fairyland and everyone lived happily ever after.

# The Tin Whistle

Once upon a time, there was a princess who lived in an old, grey castle. Everyone who lived in the castle was sad. Even the king and queen were gloomy.

The castle was filled with dusty old furniture, suits of armour and paintings of unhappy-looking ancestors. The princess found it quite funny, in fact, she was the only cheerful one in the castle. However, try as she might, the princess could never raise everyone's spirits.

Sometimes, the princess would go for a walk in her favourite part of the garden. There, in a quiet corner, was a statue of a handsome young man, dressed as a prince. The young man's face had a very sad expression and the princess often wondered what had made him so unhappy.

One day, the princess was playing near the statue when she saw something shining in its stone hand. She climbed up and found a small, golden key. "I'm sure this wasn't here before," thought the princess. "I wonder what sort of lock a key like this opens?"

The princess searched all over the gloomy castle, from the cellars to the roof. Then, in the attic, she found a chest made of ancient wood. The princess put the key in the lock and, when she turned it, the lock clicked open. Inside the chest was an old tin whistle.

The princess took the tin whistle to her room and tried to play it. She was surprised to find that her fingers flew over the holes and she was able to play a lovely tune. The princess stood up and danced round and round her room as she played.

Suddenly, as if by magic, the china ornaments in the princess' room started to twirl and dance along to the music. The princess was very surprised, but she didn't stop playing.

The princess danced down the stairs, playing the tune. The rusty suits of armour came to life and marched merrily behind her. Even the knives and forks in the kitchen began to beat time to the music. Then the plates and cups began to dance together.

In the great hall, all the chairs danced in formation and even the long, oak table began to jig around. Inside the paintings, the princess' ancestors danced and twirled. Even the stuffed moose head on the wall began to sing along, cheerfully.

"What is this noise?" asked the king, as he came marching into the hall with the queen. He grabbed the tin whistle and suddenly, all the dancing stopped. The king put the whistle in a drawer. "We'll have none of this in my castle," he said and sent the princess off to bed.

That night, the princess had a dream that she was looking out of her bedroom window at the statue in the garden. The statue seemed to be pleading with her. "Set me free," it said. "If you do not wake me tonight, I will remain stone for another one hundred years."

The princess woke up, dressed quietly and then crept downstairs. The castle guards were dozing and she slipped past them without a sound. The princess found the tin whistle in the drawer, where the king had put it, then she crept out into the moonlit garden.

Everything was still and quiet outside. The princess walked along the paths, towards the quiet spot, where the statue stood. She played softly on the tin whistle. The moonlight shone brighter and brighter on the statue of the young man and made it glow. The princess played faster and faster, until her fingers ached and she could hardly breathe.

Suddenly, the statue moved. It raised its hands and slowly, all the stone changed into living flesh. The young man stepped down from the statue and took the princess' hand.

"You have saved me," he said. "I am a prince who visited this castle one hundred years ago, to marry a princess. However, the princess' wicked and jealous stepmother cursed me to become a statue and for the castle to be forever gloomy. My only hope was that someone would find my magic whistle and use it to bring me back to life. Now the curse is broken."

As the sun came up, the castle came to life. The princess played the tin whistle and everything in the castle danced around. The prince and the princess went into the great hall to greet the king and queen.

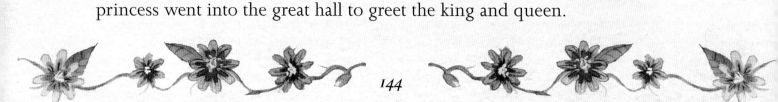

The king and queen weren't unhappy anymore. In fact, they were overjoyed to see their daughter and the prince. They smiled and hugged each other. "We have lived under this enchantment for far too long," they said. "Now that the curse has been broken, we will make this castle a happy place once more."

The prince fell in love with the princess and it wasn't long before they were married. On the day of their wedding, everyone in the castle danced and danced. The castle was filled with light and laughter and no one had any reason to be unhappy, ever again.

# Thumbelina

Once upon a time, there was a little old woman who lived all alone. She longed for a child to keep her company. One day, she met an old witch hobbling down the road, outside her cottage. "Please, help me!" cried the old woman. "I want a little child so much!" The witch pushed a tiny barley seed into the old woman's hands. "Plant this and your wish will come true."

The old woman planted the seed and watered it carefully. Soon, it grew into a little green plant, with a single flower at its tip. The flower opened and inside sat a tiny, baby girl, no bigger than a thumb.

The old woman was overjoyed. "I shall call you Thumbelina," she said. She made Thumbelina a bed from half a walnut shell and put her in it. The tiny baby smiled and went straight to sleep.

As Thumbelina got older, she never got any taller, but she was the sweetest and kindest girl in the land. She loved to play in a bowl of water that the old woman put on the table. Thumbelina used a tulip petal as a boat and two stalks of grass for oars. She rowed around and around the bowl, as happy as could be.

One night, when Thumbelina was sleeping, a slimy toad crept through an open window and saw her. "What a pretty little girl," the toad said. "She will make a perfect wife for my son." The toad picked up Thumbelina and hopped out the window. He carried Thumbelina to the cold, muddy river bank and left her on a lily pad. "Soon, you will marry my son," he said and then hopped away.

Thumbelina was very frightened and began to cry. The fish in the river felt sorry for her and gnawed at the stem of the lily pad. Then a white butterfly let Thumbelina tie a thin reed around it. The butterfly pulled the lily pad into the middle of the river, where it floated downstream, far from the horrible, slimy toad.

Suddenly, something picked Thumbelina up. It was a big, black beetle, who carried Thumbelina to his home in the woods. "What a strange-looking creature you are," said the beetle. "Why, you only have two legs and no feelers at all. It must be horrible to be so ugly."

Thumbelina ran away from the insulting beetle and made herself a little home at the edge of the woods. She pulled a big leaf over her as a roof and made herself a bed from a couple of petals that she found. All summer, she lived in peace, sipping nectar from the flowers and making friends with the animals of the wood.

Then winter came and her little home was very cold. Snow started to fall. Thumbelina was so tiny, every snowflake that fell on her head felt like a big bucketful of snow.

Thumbelina was so cold, she was nearly freezing to death. She walked to a field where a field mouse lived. "Please let me come in to your burrow," she said, "or I'll freeze!"

The kindly field mouse took her in and she spent the winter with him. Thumbelina liked the field mouse's burrow, but she didn't like the field mouse's friend, a boastful mole. "My burrow is much bigger than this," the mole said. "Thumbelina, you must come and live with me."

Thumbelina protested, but the mole wouldn't listen. He took her to his dark, clammy underground den. "Isn't it wonderful?" said the mole, but Thumbelina hated it.

One day, when Thumbelina was exploring the muddy tunnels, she found a swallow lying in the dark. He had become too cold and had fallen from the sky when he tried to fly south. Thumbelina nursed the swallow back to health, until spring arrived. "Thank you, Thumbelina," the swallow said. It fluttered out of the hole and into the sun.

The mole wouldn't let Thumbelina go outside, in case she ran away. The summer months passed and soon autumn came. "It is time for us to marry," said the mole. "Then you can live with me forever."

No matter how much Thumbelina protested, the mole wouldn't listen. One day, when Thumbelina was sitting by the entrance to the burrow crying, she heard the flutter of wings. It was the swallow. "Come with me, quickly," the swallow chirped. "We swallows are flying south before the winter comes again."

Thumbelina jumped on the swallow's back and it flew off to join its brothers in the sky. The swallows' journey south was a long one and Thumbelina fell asleep on the swallow's soft back.

When she woke up, Thumbelina found that they were in a sunlit field, filled with poppies. She had never seen such lovely flowers before. Looking closer, Thumbelina saw a strange sight. Inside every flower, sat a tiny person. Some were men and some were women and they all had shimmering wings, like dragonflies. They were no bigger than Thumbelina.

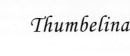

The tiny man in the flower nearest Thumbelina was very handsome. He wore a shining crown. "I am the prince of the flower spirits," he said to Thumbelina. "You are the most beautiful girl I have ever met. Will you marry me?"

Thumbelina agreed immediately. All the flower spirits brought lovely gifts to their wedding. The best was a pair of shimmering wings for Thumbelina. She and the prince spent their days flying from flower to flower together and they lived happily every after.

# The Fairy Queen

Once upon a time, a princess had three older sisters who loved to go to balls and parties. The princess wanted to go too, but she was too young. When her sisters were getting ready to go out, the youngest princess would go off by herself and walk around the fields and hills near the castle.

One day, the princess took a different path than usual and found herself in a wooded glade. The sun was setting and it would soon be dark. The princess knew she had to return home soon. Just as she was about to go back, she saw a glimmer nearby. It was coming from inside a ring of grass.

The princess walked towards the ring and saw pretty girls, who were dressed in white with red caps. They were dancing hand in hand, round the ring. The princess knew this must be a fairy ring because her grandmother had often told her about them. Suddenly, the girls called to the princess, "Come and join the dance!"

As soon as the princess stepped into the ring, she saw a fine lady on a white horse appear, as if from nowhere. The lady wore a dress that was covered in pale, gleaming jewels. Her eyes seemed to glow, just like her jewels. "I am the Fairy Queen," she said. "Won't you come with us, Princess? The party is about to start."

The princess got on the back of the white horse and they rode off to a small hill. As if by magic, the hillside opened and the horse and riders went inside.

The Fairy Queen took the princess into a strange and beautiful forest, where silver trees had fruit, like glass, hanging from their branches. The fruit gave off a pale light and the princess could see three fairy girls playing a harp, a flute and a violin. All around, fairy folk danced gracefully to the strange, enchanting music.

Fairy waiters moved around the guests, holding plates piled high with delicious-looking cakes and candy. The princess reached out to take a cake, but stopped suddenly. She remembered something her grandmother had once told her – anyone who tasted fairy food, or drink, would be trapped in Fairyland for a hundred years.

The princess danced until late in the night and then she said goodbye to the Fairy Queen. "Please, have a sip of some of our special apple juice before you go," said the Fairy Queen, handing the princess a golden goblet.

The princess refused to take the goblet. "No, thank you, Your Majesty," she said, politely. "I have had a wonderful time. You must come and visit my palace soon."
"Thank you for your invitation," said the Fairy Queen. "We will be at your castle tomorrow night, when the clock chimes eight."

There was a sudden whirl of light and sound. The fairy kingdom disappeared and the princess found herself outside her castle, just as the sun was setting. It was as if no time had passed at all. The princess tried to tell her sisters about the Fairy Queen, but they didn't believe her. "You must have been dreaming," they said.

The next night, at eight o'clock, the princess heard the sound of hooves outside the castle. The doors opened and the Fairy Queen entered the Great Hall, followed by all the fairy folk. They started to play beautiful fairy music that was strange and magical. Soon, the people of the castle were dancing, as if bewitched.

The Fairy Queen watched with a smile, while everyone whirled gracefully around. "What pretty people," the princess heard her say. "I will take them all home with me. It will be most amusing to have them in my fairy palace."

"This is my fault," thought the princess. "If I don't do something, everyone will be spirited away to Fairyland." Then the princess had an idea. She raced down to the palace kitchens. There, she found a small piece of brittle candy and made a big hole in it, so that it resembled a ring.

The princess took the candy to the Fairy Queen. "A present for you, Your Majesty," she said, slipping the ring onto the Fairy Queen's finger. But, as soon as it had touched her skin, the ring suddenly crumbled into small candy pieces.

The Fairy Queen licked her finger. "Why, that wasn't a real ring. It was made of sugar. What a strange girl you are. But enough games," said the Fairy Queen, "you are all coming with me to Fairyland."

The Fairy Queen raised her arms to spirit everyone away, but nothing happened. "Where are my powers?" she cried.
"My grandmother told me that fairy magic works both ways," said the princess. "Now that you have tasted mortal food, I'm afraid your powers are lost until you return to Fairyland."

The Fairy Queen looked furious, then amused. She nodded. "Fair is fair, Princess. We will go, but remember, the door in the hill is always open to you." Then in a flash, the fairies were all gone.

When the princess was old enough to go to the palace balls, everyone noticed that she was the finest dancer of them all. Some said it was because her sisters had taught her, but the princess knew it was because she had once danced all night with the Fairy Queen.

# Little Red Hen

Little Red Hen was pecking and clucking in the farmyard when, all of a sudden, she came upon a grain of wheat. "I could eat this wheat," she said to her friends, "or we could plant it in the ground and then maybe it will grow and feed us all."

And so she asked, "Who will help me plant this grain?"
"Not I," quacked the duck.
"Not I," honked the goose.
"Not I," mewed the cat.
"Very well," said Little Red Hen. "Then I shall plant the grain."
And so she made a little hole in a clearing and planted he grain all by herself.

# Little Red Hen

The very next day, Little Red Hen looked at the spot where she had planted the grain and saw that it was dry. And so she asked her friends, "Who will help me water this grain?"

"Not I," quacked the duck.

"Not I," honked the goose.

"Not I," mewed the cat.

"Very well," said Little Red Hen. "Then I shall water the grain."

And so she brought a watering can and gave the grain a cool drink. And she did the same the next day, and the day after that, all by herself.

Very soon, the grain had grown into tall, ripe wheat, good enough to eat. So Little Red Hen asked her friends, "Who will help me cut this wheat?"

"Not I," quacked the duck.

"Not I," honked the goose.

"Not I," mewed the cat.

"Very well," said Little Red Hen. "Then I shall cut the wheat."

And so she brought a scythe to cut the wheat and then she gathered it all up, all by herself.

# Little Red Hen

Now the wheat was ready to be ground into flour, so she asked her friends,
"Who will help me take this wheat to the miller?"
"Not I," quacked the duck.
"Not I," honked the goose.
"Not I," mewed the cat.
"Very well," said Little Red Hen. "Then I shall take the wheat to the miller."

And so she put the wheat on the cart, and she drove the cart to the mill.
The miller saw that the wheat was very good indeed, and there was enough to
make a whole sack of flour, which Little Red Hen took back to the farm all by
herself.

Now the flour was ready to be baked into bread. So Little Red Hen asked
her friends, "Who will help me bake the bread?"
"Not I," quacked the duck.
"Not I," honked the goose.

"Not I," mewed the cat.

"Very well," said Little Red Hen. "Then I shall bake the bread." And so she kneaded the dough and put it into the oven. When it smelled good and ready, she asked her friends, "Who will help me eat this bread?"

"I will," quacked the duck.

"I will," honked the goose.

"I will," mewed the cat.

"Hmmm," said Little Red Hen. "No one would help me plant the grain, water it, cut the wheat, take it to the miller or bake the flour into bread. But everyone will eat it?" she asked.

"Yes," quacked the duck.

"Yes," honked the goose.

"Yes," mewed the cat.

"I don't think so," said Little Red Hen, and she ate up the bread – all by herself.

# The Princess and the Ballerina

Once upon a time, a princess named Rosalind lived in a huge palace with her mother, the queen, and her father, the king. Princess Rosalind loved to dance. All day long, she would twirl and whirl around the palace, standing on tiptoe to show her parents that she was just like a proper ballerina. However, no matter how well Rosalind danced, the king and queen never noticed her. They were always busy doing other things around the palace. However, Rosalind was determined that she would dance like a real ballerina.

One day, a troupe of ballet dancers came to the palace to perform for the king. Rosalind was allowed to go and watch them in the Great Hall. The stage was set and the lights went down. Rosalind felt a thrill of excitement as the ballerinas whirled onto the stage and the performance began.

The dancers moved around the stage with beauty and grace. They leaped and spun, as if they were lighter than air. Their dresses shimmered like diamonds in the light. Rosalind was enchanted. At the end of the performance, the dancers bowed and the audience applauded. Some people even stood up and called "Bravo".

# The Princess and the Ballerina

One ballerina, who danced like an angel, got the most applause. She wore a jewelled mask over her face and had flowers in her hair.

"She must be the luckiest girl in the world," thought Rosalind, enviously. "Everyone loves her. I must meet her."

Nobody noticed Rosalind, as she sneaked behind the stage, where the dancers were busy changing out of their costumes. Rosalind found the ballerina taking off her mask. Her name was Ella and she was pale and thin. Like the princess, she had long, golden hair.

"Nobody notices me," said Rosalind. "I wish I could dance on stage, like you. Then everyone would finally see me."

"I wish I were a princess like you," said Ella. "Then I would be able to lounge on golden cushions and eat delicious food all day."

The two girls looked at each other and smiled. They both had the same idea. "Let's swap places!" they cried.

The next night, before the dancers' last performance at the palace, the princess and the ballerina met up and changed clothes. "We leave tonight," said Ella. "We must meet later and swap back, or there will be terrible trouble."

Princess Rosalind put on Ella's costume and the jewelled mask. Ella put on the princess' pretty pink dress. The ballerina's mask meant that none of the other dancers noticed that the princess wasn't Ella. She tiptoed off to the palace and sure enough, nobody even glanced at her.

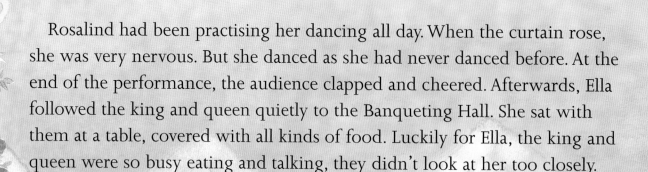

Rosalind had been practising her dancing all day. When the curtain rose, she was very nervous. But she danced as she had never danced before. At the end of the performance, the audience clapped and cheered. Afterwards, Ella followed the king and queen quietly to the Banqueting Hall. She sat with them at a table, covered with all kinds of food. Luckily for Ella, the king and queen were so busy eating and talking, they didn't look at her too closely.

Ella had never seen such delicious food. She started eating before everyone else. She grabbed handfuls of grapes and ate a chicken drumstick with her hands, instead of using her gold knife and fork. When she drank milk, she got it all around her mouth. Then, without using a napkin, she wiped her mouth with her hand. The king and queen were shocked. "Rosalind, where are your manners?" the queen said. "Go straight to bed!"

Ella was marched upstairs to Rosalind's room. The queen was angry and locked the door, so Ella couldn't get out. Outside, the dancers' caravans were getting ready to move off. Ella could see them from her window. She had to reach them, or she would be left behind.

Ella opened the window of the bedroom and saw that she wasn't very high off the ground. She climbed out of the window and onto a ledge. The ledge was very thin, but Ella was used to balancing on her tiptoes. She looked for a way down into the gardens below.

Meanwhile, the dancers hadn't noticed that they were hiding a princess. "Ella, your dancing was a little sloppy tonight," said Ella's mother. "You will spend two hours practising tonight before you have any supper. Then we leave the palace. Tomorrow, we perform at a castle far away."

Rosalind knew she had to escape back to her family, but she was surrounded by all the dancers and Ella's mother was watching. Luckily, they were inside the grounds of the castle and the princess knew all the secret passageways that led in and out of the palace. When no one was looking, she pressed a hidden button and a small door opened.

Rosalind slipped through the door and went down a secret passage that led into the palace garden. There, she saw Ella, balancing on the window ledge. Rosalind could almost reach out and grab her. "You'll have to jump, Ella," she said "Don't worry, I'll catch you."

Ella dropped down from the ledge and Rosalind caught her. The two girls rolled onto the grass, laughing. Then they stood up and quickly swapped their clothes. "Being a princess is harder than it looks," said Ella. "Not as hard as being a dancer," laughed Rosalind.

By now, Ella's mother and the king and queen realised that their daughters were missing. They heard the girls' laughter and ran into the garden. "Ella, we're leaving," said her mother, "come on!" The princess and the ballerina smiled at each other and said goodbye.

The king and queen took Rosalind back into the palace. "I think we should spend more time together, Rosalind," said the queen. "Perhaps you could show us your dancing," added the king.

Ella's mother decided that her daughter spent far too much time dancing. "In future, Ella," she said, "you shall have more time to play."

After that, the princess and the ballerina were both much happier. Nobody ever found out that the ballerina had joined a royal banquet, or that the princess had danced on stage and they all lived happily ever after.

# Chicken Little

Chicken Little was wandering through the woods one day when PLOP, something small and hard fell onto her head. "Ouch," said Chicken Little. "That felt like the sky was falling." But the sky was not falling. What Chicken Little had felt was an acorn falling from a tree, although she didn't know that.

On through the woods went Chicken Little when PLOP, something else fell on her head. "Ouch," she cried. "That really, really felt like the sky was falling." But of course, it was another acorn falling from a tree, although Chicken Little didn't know that.

She kept on walking when PLOP! PLOP! PLOP! Three acorns fell on her head all at once. "Help!" yelled Chicken Little. "The sky really is falling!"

As she was rushing along, she bumped into Henny Penny,
who was out for a stroll.
"Help!" said Chicken Little to Henny Penny, "the sky is falling!"
"Where?" asked Henny Penny, looking around in shock.
"Right on my head," said Chicken Little. "We must go to tell the King."
So, Chicken Little and Henny Penny set out to tell the King.

On the way, they met Ducky Lucky, who was going to the pond.
"Help!" said Henny Penny to Ducky Lucky. "The sky is falling!"
"Where?" asked Ducky Lucky, looking around in shock.
"Right on Chicken Little's head," said Henny Penny.
"We must go to tell the King."
So Chicken Little, Henny Penny and Ducky Lucky set out to tell the King.

On the way, they met Cocky Locky, who was going to the barnyard.
"Help!" said Ducky Lucky to Cocky Locky. "The sky is falling!"
"Where?" asked Cocky Locky, looking around in shock.
"Right on Chicken Little's head," said Ducky Lucky.
"We must go to tell the King."
So Chicken Little, Henny Penny, Ducky Lucky and Cocky Locky set out
to tell the king.

# Chicken Little

On the way, they met Goosey Lucy, who was going to the market.
"Help!" said Cocky Locky to Goosey Lucy. "The sky is falling!"
"Where?" asked Goosey Lucy, looking around in shock.
"Right on Chicken Little's head," said Cocky Locky. "We must go to tell
the King." So Chicken Little, Henny Penny, Ducky Lucky, Cocky Locky and
Goosey Lucy set out to tell the King.

On the way, they met Turkey Lurkey, who was going to the meadow.
"Help!" said Goosey Lucy to Turkey Lurkey. "The sky is falling!"
"Where?" asked Turkey Lurkey, looking around in shock.
"Right on Chicken Little's head," said Goosey Lucy. "We must go to tell the
King." So Chicken Little, Henny Penny, Ducky Lucky, Cocky Locky, Goosey
Lucy and Turkey Lurkey set out to tell the King.

# Chicken Little

On the way, they met Foxy Loxy, who was going to his den.
"Help!" said Turkey Lurkey to Foxy Loxy. "The sky is falling!"
Where?" asked Foxy Loxy, looking around in shock.
"Right on Chicken Little's head," said Turkey Lurkey. "We must go tell the King."

But Foxy Loxy said that if the sky was falling, they would be safer waiting in his den until the danger was over. So Chicken Little, Henny Penny, Ducky Lucky, Cocky Locky, Goosey Lucy and Tuzrkey Lurkey all followed Foxy Loxy into his den.

But of course it was not safe in the den and the danger was far from over, for Foxy Loxy gobbled up Chicken Little, Henny Penny, Ducky Lucky, Cocky Locky, Goosey Lucy and Turkey Lurkey. And the King never did find out that the sky was falling.

# Trouble

On the morning of her seventh birthday, Katie awoke to find the cutest little kitten she had ever seen, sitting at the foot of her bed. The kitten was watching her with a curious look in his eyes. "Hello!" said Katie. "What's your name?"

But the kitten just looked at her mischievously.

"Happy Birthday!" said Katie's mother, from the doorway.
"He doesn't have a name yet. We thought you would like to decide."
"Thanks!" said Katie, leaping out of bed and giving her mother a huge hug.
"He's just what I've been wishing for!"

Katie and the kitten bonded instantly. Though Katie received lots of other lovely gifts for her birthday, nothing compared to the little bundle of fur that bounced around the room.
"You need a name," said Katie, kissing the little kitten on his nose. But, try as she might, she couldn't decide what to call him. With her parents' help, she made a list of ideas – Cookie, Ginger, Fluffy – but none of the names were quite right.

When it was time to get ready for bed, Katie sat and brushed her hair, while the kitten lay on her bed and licked his paws.
"Have you thought of a name for your kitten yet?" asked Katie's mother, coming in. Katie shook her head.

# Trouble

"Why don't you think overnight?" suggested Katie's mother. "I'm sure you'll have thought of one by tomorrow. Now, it's time for him to come downstairs so you can go to bed."

"But he wants to sleep in here with me!" Katie protested. "He told me so!"

"The decision is final," Katie's mother replied. "He'll sleep fine downstairs in the hall in his snug new basket," she promised.

But nobody got a wink of sleep that night, especially not the kitten. All night long he mewed and mewed and mewed. In the morning, Katie's parents decided that they would have to move the kitten into the living room. "Perhaps it was too cold for him in the hall," said her mother. "At least if he is in the living room, the noise will be muffled, so he won't keep everyone awake."

Katie cuddled the kitten and stroked his fur. "I'm sorry," she whispered in his ear. "I know all you want is to sleep in my room."

The kitten looked up at Katie and purred.
"Worst of all," said Katie, tickling his ears,
"I still can't think of a name for you!"

That night, Katie's mother put the kitten's basket into the living room.

Katie woke up to sound of her mother shouting. Quick as a flash, she raced downstairs.
"Oh no, little kitten!" she cried. "What have you done now?"

All over the sofa were rips and tears, and little kitten claw marks.
It was ruined.
"Right!" said Katie's father. "From now on, that kitten is sleeping in the kitchen by the back door."
"But Dad," cried Katie, "why can't he just sleep in my room? He won't cause any trouble, I promise!"

But Katie's parents were in no mood to listen, and so the kitten's basket was moved to the kitchen.

# Trouble

The next morning, Katie rushed downstairs to check on the little kitten. "Oh no!" she cried, gazing around the kitchen in horror. It looked like an elephant had been let loose. There was food and mess everywhere!

Katie's parents were annoyed at the mess, but concerned, too. "How much trouble can one little kitten cause?" said Mother, picking up the remains of Dad's newspaper. "If he doesn't start behaving himself, we may have to think about finding a new home for him."
"Please don't send him away!" cried Katie. "I think he's just lonely. If you let him sleep in my room, I'm sure he'll be as good as gold."
"It's worth a try," said Katie's dad. "But just for tonight. If he makes any mess, or keeps us awake, then I'm afraid he'll have to go."

## Trouble

So that night, the kitten's basket was put in Katie's room. And before they went to sleep Katie talked sternly to the kitten.

"You must try your very hardest to be good tonight," she told him, "otherwise you will be in real trouble." She also promised him that if he was good, then she would definitely think of a name for him in the morning. The kitten just looked at her and purred, but Katie was sure that he had understood.

In the morning, her mother opened Katie's bedroom door very gingerly. "Goodness me!" she exclaimed.

Katie and the kitten were on the bed playing – and there wasn't a single sign of a mess.

"He was as good as gold all night," cried Katie. "Can he stay?"

"Of course," her mother said with a smile, "as long as he behaves and keeps out of trouble."

"That's it!" said Katie with a huge grin on her face. "That's the perfect name for him. I'll call him Trouble!"

# The Flower Princess

Once upon a time, a beautiful princess lived in a palace with a magnificent garden. In the summer, the garden burst into life. In the winter, it sparkled with snow and ice. Springtime brought blooms and blossoms of every kind and all who saw them were amazed. At the heart of the garden, stood the tallest tree in the land.

More than anything else, the princess loved to spend time digging and planting flowers. Many rich princes came to try and win her hand in marriage, but she ignored them and tended her plants instead.

Every day, a young gardener helped the princess. He was in love with her, but she was so dazzled by the beauty of the flowers in the garden, she hardly noticed him.

Eventually, the king and queen decided it was time for their daughter to marry and invited two rich princes to visit. One prince was very fat and nervous-looking and the other prince was thin and delicate. They went to speak to the princess, who was outside, near the tallest tree.

"If I must marry, I must," said the princess, wiping her hands on her apron. "But I have one request. I will marry the man who can climb this tree and bring me the single blossom that grows at its highest point."

The two princes looked up at the tree. It was so high that they could hardly see the top of it. The blossom was just a flash of pink in the sky. There weren't many low branches on the tree, either. It was going to be very difficult to climb. But the princes both wanted to marry the princess, because they knew that, whoever married her, would one day be king.

The fat prince was the first to speak. "I will climb the tree and fetch the blossom," he declared, then he clambered awkwardly up into the lower branches.

By the time he got halfway up the tree, the fat prince was red-faced and out of breath. Trying not to fall, he scrambled up to the very top and found the pink blossom. Beside the blossom, sat a big, golden eagle. The eagle had great, curved claws and a sharp, dangerous-looking beak. The prince was so frightened, he scampered back down the tree as fast as he could. Then he quickly said goodby and left the palace forever.

The next day, the thin prince tried to climb the tree. He was much stronger and fitter than the fat prince and was glad that the princess was there to see him. He slung ropes on to the branches and climbed them speedily, until he was almost at the top. The eagle stared down at him with its hard, gold eyes.

"What do you seek?" asked the eagle.

"I seek the blossom," replied the thin prince.

"Why do you seek it?" the eagle asked.

"So that I can become king, one day," said the thin prince.

"That was the wrong answer," cawed the eagle. It launched itself at the thin prince and chased him all the way down the tree, out of the garden and away from the palace for good.

The princess began to cry. She was very sad that neither of the princes had brought her the blossom. "It is so beautiful," she said, sadly. "I would have loved to smell its perfume and feel its delicate petals.

The young gardener overheard the princess and decided to get the blossom for her. He put his tools down and began to climb the tree. Without any ropes to help him, it was a hard climb.

When he reached the top of the tree, the eagle spread its wings and stared at him sternly. "What do you seek?" it asked.

"The blossom, please," replied the gardener.

"Why do you seek it?" asked the eagle.

The gardener thought for a moment and then he spoke. "I am just a simple gardener," he said. However, I love the princess more than anyone in the world. Her heart was set on having this blossom and neither of the princes were able to get it for her. Now she is sad and all I want to do is to make her happy."

"That is the right answer," said the eagle. "Now climb onto my back and take the blossom."

The gardener climbed on the eagle's back and picked the pink blossom. As soon as he did, the eagle began to magically grow in size, until it was gigantic. Suddenly, the eagle spread its great wings and glided down, to the bottom of the tree, where the princess stood.

The princess couldn't believe her eyes. She was amazed to see the gardener, flying on the giant eagle's back, holding the blossom. She blushed as he knelt and gave it to her. It was then that the princess realised something. "I have loved you all along, my kind and brave gardener," she said.

The princess and the gardener were married soon after. Every day, they continued to work in the garden together. When they became king and queen, they covered the whole kingdom with beautiful flowers.

# The Flower Princess

# The Three Little Pigs

Once upon a time, there were three little pigs who wanted to leave home. "We must build our own houses," they said. The three little pigs said goodbye to their mother and set off.

The first little pig hadn't walked very far when he met a man carrying a bale of straw. The little pig bought the bale of straw and started to build a house. When he was finished, the first little pig had a house of straw. It had a straw door, straw walls and straw windows.

The second little pig met a man carrying a great bundle of sticks. The little pig bought the sticks and made himself a house of sticks. It was stronger than the house of straw and the second little pig was very proud of it.

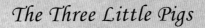

The third little pig walked a long way and came upon a man carrying lots of bricks. The little pig bought the bricks and built himself a house that was very strong and sturdy.

The little pigs didn't know it, but they were being watched by a hungry wolf, who loved to eat little pigs. He went to the house of straw and knocked on the door.

"Little pig, little pig, let me come in," said the wolf.

"Not by the hair on my chinny-chin-chin!" said the first little pig.

"Then I'll huff and I'll puff and I'll blow your house down!" cried the wolf.

And he huffed and he puffed and he blew the straw house down.

The poor little pig squealed and ran all the way to his brother's house made of sticks. He ran inside, just before the wolf knocked on the door.

"Little pig, little pig, let me come in," growled the wolf.

"Not by the hair on my chinny-chin-chin!" said the second little pig.

"Then I'll huff and I'll puff and I'll blow your house down!" said the wolf.

And he huffed and he puffed and he blew the little stick house down.

The two little pigs ran as fast as they could to the house of the third little pig. As soon as they were inside and had bolted the door, they heard a loud knocking.

"Little pig, little pig, let me come in!" said the wolf.
"Not by the hair on my chinny-chin-chin!" said the third little pig.
"Then I'll huff and I'll puff and I'll blow your house down!" said the wolf.
So he huffed and he puffed, but nothing happened!

The wolf huffed and puffed again, but still nothing happened. The third little pig's house of bricks was too sturdy and the wolf couldn't blow it down.

The wolf was out of breath, but hungrier than ever. "I'll have to trick those pigs into leaving the house," he thought. So, the wolf put on his kindest voice and tapped on the door. "You will get hungry soon, little piggies and I don't mean you any harm. Won't you come and pick some turnips with me tomorrow, at six o'clock?"

Now, the third little pig knew that the wolf wanted to eat him and his brothers, so he thought of a way to outwit him. "We'd love to pick turnips with you," he said. "Please call again tomorrow, at six o'clock."

The next day, the three little pigs tiptoed out of the house at five o'clock. They gathered all the turnips from the nearby field. Then they tiptoed back to the house. At six o'clock, the wolf knocked on the door. "Time to get turnips, little piggies!" he growled, softly.

"You're late!" shouted the third little pig. "Sorry, but we've already got the turnips!" Inside the brick house, the three little pigs were all laughing at the wolf.

The wolf was very cross, but he wasn't about to be beaten by three silly, little pigs, so he thought of another plan. "There are some juicy apples in the orchard nearby. Come with me tomorrow, at five o'clock, and I will help you pick some," he said. The little pigs agreed to meet the wolf, but first, they set about making a big pot of boiling turnip soup.
"This will come in very handy," said the third little pig.

The next day, the little pigs tiptoed out of the house at four o'clock and ran to the orchard. "We will make a fool of that silly, old wolf," they giggled, as they picked the juicy, green apples.

But the wily wolf had guessed what the pigs were up to and he went to the orchard early, too. He found the three little pigs with a big basket of apples, all ready to go home. He growled and chased them out of the orchard, all the way back to the brick house, but the pigs got inside just in time.

Now the wolf was really angry. He snarled and jumped onto the roof of the little brick house. "Little pigs," he growled, "I'm going to eat you all up!" Then he jumped down the chimney.

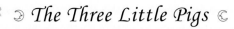

But the wolf didn't know that, at the bottom of the chimney, was the pot of turnip soup. He fell into it with a great big SPLASH and got such a fright, he ran away and never bothered the little pigs ever again.

The three little pigs were very happy to be free of the big, bad, wolf. The third little pig built his two brothers brand new houses made of bricks, just like his own — and they all lived safely and happily ever after.

# The China Pony

Once upon a time, there was a girl named Snowdrop who lived with her father in a tiny, tumbledown cottage on the side of a high mountain. One day, a strange old woman arrived at their cottage. "I am your long-lost aunt," she said. "I have travelled a great distance to come and take care of you."

But the aunt was nasty. When Snowdrop's father wasn't looking, she would scold and snap at Snowdrop and make her scrub the floors, wash the dishes and clean all the clothes.

One morning, Snowdrop woke to find her aunt standing over her. "Your father has had to go away," said the aunt, sternly. "Now get up, you lazy girl. There are chores to be done."

From then on, Snowdrop was always unhappy. Her aunt made her go to the nearby village and buy all the best food. But, when she returned, her aunt would eat it all and only toss Snowdrop a crust of bread. She even made Snowdrop sleep outside in the freezing cold. Snowdrop often thought of running away. "But what if my father comes back and I'm gone?" she would think. "It would break his heart."

## The China Pony

One day, when she was buying food in the village shop, Snowdrop saw a small white china pony on the shelf. "How much is the pony?" she asked the shopkeeper, but he didn't know.
"I've never seen it before," the shopkeeper said. "Please, take it. Maybe it was meant for you."

Snowdrop took the china pony home. She was afraid that if her aunt saw the pony, she would take it away. So Snowdrop hid it under her pillow.

In the middle of the night, Snowdrop woke up to find something nuzzling her face. It was a beautiful, white pony "I am the china pony," it said. "Come, sit on my back."

Snowdrop climbed onto the pony's back. Suddenly, they were outside, "I am here to help you rescue your father," said the pony. "The old woman is not really your aunt at all. She is an evil sorceress and she has imprisoned him in a castle, guarded by an ogre."

"The castle is many days' travel from here, on a tower of rock that cannot be climbed," said the pony. "And when the sun rises today, the ogre will eat your father."

Snowdrop wept. "Oh, china pony, is there nothing you can do?"
"There may be one thing," replied the pony. "On the mountain, a single golden flower grows. It is said to grant the power of flight. We could use this flower to help your father escape. However, nobody has ever found it."

Snowdrop and the pony spent all night on the cold mountainside, looking for the golden flower, but they found nothing. Exhausted, Snowdrop lay down in the snow. The dawn was breaking and as the first rays of the sun hit the mountainside, Snowdrop saw a golden glow in the snow. It was the golden flower!

"We do not have much time," said the horse. "When the sun is up, the ogre will eat your father."
Snowdrop picked the flower and the horse ate it. Snowdrop got on the pony's back and it leaped from the mountain top. But it didn't fall. Instead, it flew through the sky.

Snowdrop and the china pony flew through the air and landed at the
bottom of the castle, just before the sun was in the sky. "The ogre's tower has
three levels," said the pony. "On each level, there is a chest full of treasure.
Do not touch it, but go straight past."

So Snowdrop entered the castle. On the first level, there was a chest full of
gold coins, but Snowdrop passed it by. On the second level, there was a chest
twice as big, filled with diamonds, rubies and emeralds. But Snowdrop
didn't touch any of them.

Snowdrop ran up the stairs to the third level of the castle. An enormous
chest lay in the middle of the room, filled to the brim with gold, beautiful
jewellery and sparkling stones.

Behind the chest, an ugly, green ogre was snoring loudly. In the corner of the tower, chained to the wall, was Snowdrop's father.

Snowdrop tiptoed up to the ogre. She saw a large key tucked into his belt. Carefully, she slid the key out of the belt and unlocked the chains. Snowdrop's father was overjoyed to see her.

As they made their way silently toward the staircase, Snowdrop's foot touched a jewel that had fallen out of the treasure chest. Suddenly, the chest slammed shut and the ogre awoke. It looked around, bleary-eyed and said in a thunderous voice, "Who is stealing my treasure?" The ogre saw Snowdrop and her father disappearing down the staircase. It let out a terrible roar and thundered after them.

Snowdrop and her father ran downstairs as quickly as they could. Behind them, they could hear the fierce ogre thudding down the steps with his great, clumsy feet.

Outside, Snowdrop pushed her father onto the pony and she jumped on behind him. The ogre almost reached them when the white pony lifted off into the air and flew far away from the ogre and the castle.

However, Snowdrop's aunt, the wicked sorceress, sent thunder and lightning to knock them from the sky, but the white pony was too fast. He avoided every blast and kicked the lightning with his hooves, sending it crashing back to hit the sorceress, who disappeared in shower of sparks.

The white pony landed safely outside the tiny, tumbledown cottage. Snowdrop and her father climbed down and hugged one another. They turned to thank the china pony, but it was gone. In its place was a handsome prince.

"I was enchanted by the sorceress," he explained. "She turned me into a china ornament by day and a white pony by night. Now she is dead, the enchantment is lifted and I can ask for Snowdrop's hand in marriage. It wasn't long before the prince and Snowdrop were married and they were never bothered by the wicked enchantress again.

# The Golden Goose

Once upon a time, there were three brothers. The two older brothers were clever and strong, but the youngest was small and shy. The rest of the family teased him and called him names.

One day, their father told them he needed some wood from the forest for the fire. The oldest and strongest brother jumped up.

"Father, let me go," he said. "I am the strongest and the smartest. I will go into the forest and bring back more wood than you'll ever need!"

So his mother gave the brother a loaf of freshly baked bread and a bottle of good wine. "Take these," she told him. "You will need something to nourish you and quench your thirst."

When the oldest brother reached the forest, he met an old man.

"Good day to you, young sir," called the old man. "I am famished. Do you have any bread?"

"Yes," replied the brother, "but I need it for my own lunch. I cannot spare any."

"In that case," said the man, "do you have anything to drink? I have had nothing all day!"

"I'm sorry," said the brother. "I would give you some wine, but I need it for myself. Chopping wood is thirsty work. Now, if you don't mind, I'm very busy, so I must be on my way!"

"It is a shame you cannot spare anything for me. Remember this if something happens to you," replied the old man mysteriously.

The oldest brother marched off into the forest and found a fine tree to chop. He had not been working long when CHIP! CHOP! OUCH! His hand slipped, and the axe cut him.

"Oh! Oh! My poor finger!" he cried. And he picked up his axe and ran home, wondering all the way if the strange old man had something to do with the accident.

The next day, the second brother went to his father.

"Father," he said, "I feel it is my duty as your second-born son to take up the work my poor injured brother could not finish yesterday." So he too was given a lunch of fresh bread and wine, and off he went to the forest to chop wood.

# The Golden Goose

When he reached the forest, the second brother met the same old man.

"Good day to you, young sir," smiled the old man. "Could you spare some of your lunch for a hungry old man?"

The second brother thought for a second. "I do have some bread," he replied, "but I surely cannot spare any, for I don't want to starve myself!" "Then maybe a little of your wine to ease my thirst?" asked the old man. "If you drink it, what shall I have when I am thirsty from chopping wood?" replied the second brother. "I'm sorry. You'll have to find some of your own. Now, if you will excuse me, I have work to do."
"It is a shame you cannot spare anything for me. Remember this if something should happen to you," the old man replied . . .

With that, the brother marched off into the forest, and began work. CHIP! CHOP! OUCH! The axe slipped and struck him on the foot. He let out a howl and he cursed the strange little man, for he was sure that this accident was his doing. Then he hopped all the way home!

# The Golden Goose

The next day, the youngest of the three brothers went to his father. "Let me go to chop wood for the fire," he said. "My brothers are in no state to work, and so it falls to me to finish the job."

The older brothers mocked their younger sibling, and laughed that he would be too weak to chop the wood. But the family needed the wood, and so the youngest brother was sent on his way. There was no fresh bread left, and his older brothers had drunk all the wine, so all he was given was a piece of stale crust, and a flask of water from the well.

When the youngest brother reached the edge of the forest, he too met the little old man.
"Would you share your lunch with me?" the old man asked the boy.
"I only have stale old bread and water," replied the youngest brother, "but you are welcome to share it."

The old man thanked him. And when the boy took out the bread, it was as fresh as the morning it had been baked. What was more, the water had turned into sweet wine.

As they sat and ate, the old man turned to the boy. "Because you have been kind to me, I will tell you a secret," he said, pointing to an old, withered tree. "Chop down that tree, and you will find something underneath it."

So the youngest of the brothers took the axe and swung at the old tree until it fell.

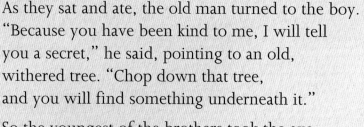

210

# The Golden Goose

There, sitting among the roots, was a goose with feathers of pure gold.

The youngest brother knew that if he returned home, the goose would be taken away from him, so he found an inn where he could stay. The innkeeper had three daughters, and when they saw the goose, each one secretly decided they would wait for the right moment and then pluck one of the golden feathers.

Later that evening, when the boy was sleeping, the eldest of the daughters crept into his room and seized the goose. But when she tried to pull her hand away, she found that she could not remove a single feather. She was stuck fast!

Next came the second daughter, looking for a feather to pinch. But the very moment she touched her sister, she also became stuck!

The third sister came in soon after, and thought she had chanced upon a game the other girls were playing. She ran to her sisters, and before they had time to warn her, she too was completely stuck!

The next morning, the boy awoke to find the innkeeper's three daughters attached to the golden goose. To teach them a lesson, he picked up the goose and marched right out of the door, so that the daughters had to follow him wherever he decided to go.

As he marched them through the streets of the village, they passed the church. "Dear me," cried the priest, who was standing outside. "What a shameful thing it is to see three girls chasing some poor boy through our little village. Let go of him, I beg you." And he reached out to pull at the youngest daughter's sleeve as they passed by.

But as the priest grabbed hold of her, he too became stuck fast by the goose's magic, and so was forced to run behind them.

# The Golden Goose

The youngest son led the procession out of the village and into the fields, where they passed two farmers.

When the priest saw these big, strong men, he called out to them. "Please help! I'm stuck! Perhaps the two of you could pull me free?"

So the farmers ran over and took hold of the priest. But as soon as they did so, they too became fixed and had to follow wherever they were led.

Soon the boy reached the city. The King who ruled the city had a beautiful daughter who was very sad. No one could cheer her up. In desperation, the King had put forth an order saying that any man who could make his daughter happy could have her hand in marriage.

# The Golden Goose

As soon as the youngest of the brothers heard this, he went directly to the royal court, followed by the innkeeper's three daughters, the priest and the two farmers, of course.

When the King's daughter witnessed this strange procession, she immediately burst into peals of laughter! The King, however, did not like the look of this silly boy and his goose, and changed his mind about the promise he had made.

"You can only marry my daughter if you bring him a man who can eat a mountain of bread," he told him.

So the boy went back to the forest where he had first found the goose. There he found the little old man, sitting on a tree stump, as before. "I am so hungry, I could eat a mountain!" cried the old man, rubbing his tummy. "Do you know where I can find more food?"

"I do," replied the boy. And he took the old man back to the royal court, where a huge mountain of bread had been baked.

The old man ate and ate and ate.

# The Golden Goose

By the end of the day the mountain was gone, and the old man had disappeared. Still the King was not satisfied.

"If you want to marry my daughter you must bring me a ship that can sail on land and water!" he demanded, certain this time that the boy would fail.

But the boy was wiser than he looked. "The old man has helped me twice," he thought to himself. "Why not a third time?"

So he returned to the forest to find the old man. Sure enough, he found him waiting in a clearing.

"Because you are kind and generous, I will help you one last time," said the old man. In a flash there was a huge ship with wheels and sails, standing right next to them!

The youngest brother climbed aboard and sailed the ship across fields and lakes, meadows and rivers, all the way back to the city.

When the King saw this, he couldn't believe his eyes. But he knew there was nothing he could do. Reluctantly, he agreed at last to the marriage.

And so the youngest son, who was once teased and made fun of, married a princess and became a royal prince. In time, the young couple inherited the kingdom. The brothers and parents of the youngest son begged his forgiveness for teasing him, and the son, being generous of heart, invited them to live in his kingdom. And so they all lived happily with each other for many years after.

# Twelve Dancing Princesses

A king once had twelve daughters. They were good daughters, except for one, very strange thing. Every night, the princesses left their shoes by their beds. Every morning, the shoes would be completely worn out. Whenever the king asked the princesses why this was, they giggled and ran off.

The king spent so much money on new shoes for his daughters, that the kingdom began to run out of money. The king decided that something had to be done. He issued a proclamation throughout the land, "Whoever can find out what happens to my daughters' shoes will become heir to the throne. He may also marry any of my daughters. But whoever fails to find out the secret in three days, will be banished."

One brave knight after another, vowed to find out the secret of the twelve dancing princesses. They tried to stay up all night, but when the sun came up, each one found that he had drifted into a deep sleep. The shoes were worn out and there was no clue as to how it had happened. These knights were banished, just as the king had promised.

One day, a soldier returned to the kingdom after a long time away.
When he heard about the proclamation, he went to the king. "I will find out
the princesses' secret," said the soldier. "I have spent my life fighting. A few
princesses don't scare me."

While the soldier was walking back from the palace to his cottage, he met
an old, wise woman and told her of his quest. "Here," said the wise woman,
holding out her hands. "Take this cloak."
"What cloak?" asked the soldier.
"It is a cloak of invisibility," said the wise woman.

The soldier held the invisible cloak. Even though he couldn't see it, he could feel its soft material in his hands. "Pretend to be asleep when the princesses call you," said the wise woman. "Then, put on the cloak. However, make sure you don't eat, or drink anything they give you."

The next night, after the princesses had got ready for bed, the soldier stood guard over them. "Take this drink," said the eldest princess, handing the soldier a goblet. "It will warm you through the night." The soldier pretended to drink from the goblet, but he secretly poured it away and pretended to fall fast asleep.

The princesses sat up in bed and looked at the soldier. "Quick," said the eldest princess. "Let's go!" She opened a trap door in the floor and the princesses put on their shoes and went through it. Quickly slipping on the cloak of invisibility, the soldier followed them.

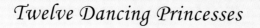

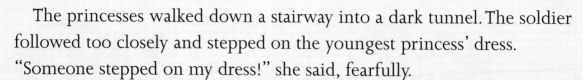

The princesses walked down a stairway into a dark tunnel. The soldier followed too closely and stepped on the youngest princess' dress. "Someone stepped on my dress!" she said, fearfully.

"Nonsense," said the eldest princess. "Hurry up, the princes are waiting."

The tunnel opened out into a wonderful land, filled with shining trees. As they passed through, the soldier saw that the leaves on the trees were made of silver. The soldier broke off a silver twig and the youngest princess heard the sound. "There is someone here," she said again, but the others told her not to be so silly.

Next, the princesses passed through a land where the trees had leaves made of gold. Then they visited a third land, where the trees had leaves of solid diamonds. The soldier had to shade his eyes, because the trees were so dazzling.

The princesses arrived at a wide, underground lake. There, twelve fairy princes, wearing glittering clothes, waited in twelve little boats. They rowed the princesses across the great lake. The soldier hid in the youngest princess' boat. No one noticed him because the magic cloak made him invisible.

When they reached the far shore, the soldier saw that they had travelled to Fairyland. Music started up from unseen instruments and the princes and the princesses danced all night. When they were tired, they drank from golden goblets.

At last, it was time to return. The soldier made sure he got back to the bedroom first. When the princesses arrived, the soldier pretended to be snoring. "It's a shame that this soldier must be banished when he fails to find out our secret," said the eldest, "but we have been bewitched and there is nothing we can do."

The next night, the soldier followed the princesses again. This time, he took a twig from one of the golden trees. On the third and last night, the soldier followed them and took a twig from a diamond tree. While the princesses danced, the soldier took a goblet and brought it back with him. The next day, the soldier came to the king. "Tell me the princesses' secret," the king said, "or I will banish you like the rest."

"The princesses have been bewitched by twelve fairy princes," said the soldier. When he showed the king and the princesses the twigs and the goblet, the spell on the princesses was broken. The king was no longer angry and hugged his daughters to him. "You may choose any of my daughters to marry," he said to the soldier.

The soldier thought for a long time. "The eldest is my choice," he said. "She is the cleverest of them all."
The eldest princess married the soldier gladly and they lived happily ever after.

# The Elves
# and the Shoemaker

Once there was a shoe shop that sold the most fabulous shoes. People came from far and wide to buy shoes from this shop; it was world famous!

But the shoemaker had not always been so successful. In fact, he had once been so poor he had lost almost everything he owned and had just enough material left to make one last pair of shoes!

He laid out his tools and leather ready for the morning and said to his wife, "Tomorrow I shall make my last pair of shoes and then what will we do?" "Do not worry, my dear," said his wife. "We are good people. We shall find a way."

When the shoemaker awoke the very next morning, he couldn't believe his eyes. Sitting on his workbench was a beautiful pair of shoes!

He looked closer and saw that the shoes were put together perfectly, with every single stitch in the right place! The shoemaker and his wife didn't know what to think, but before they had time to figure it out, there was a knock at the door.

The shoemaker opened it to see a man standing outside.
"I am sorry for calling so early," said the man, "but I have been on the road all night and my shoes are worn out! I don't suppose you have a new pair you could sell me?"

So the shoemaker showed the customer the brand-new pair of shoes.

The customer loved them and they fitted him perfectly! He paid the shoemaker a handsome price for the shoes.

With the money he had earned, the shoemaker went out and bought the materials he needed to make two more pairs of shoes.

That evening the shoemaker laid out all his work again, as he had done the night before. Once again when he woke the next morning, there, sitting on the workbench, were two brand-new pairs of shoes!

# The Elves and the Shoemaker

The shoemaker and his wife were astonished! Who on earth could have made these wonderful shoes?

Then once again they heard a knock at the door. They opened it to two men.

"Please excuse us for our rudeness," they said. "Our good friend visited us yesterday wearing what could only be described as the most glorious shoes we have ever seen! We simply had to come and see for ourselves the shop that sells these shoes! And would you perhaps have any for sale?"

So the shoemaker showed the customers in. They tried on the new shoes, and once again they fitted perfectly. This time the customers paid double! The shoemaker once again bought materials and got everything ready for the next day's work. Once more the shoes were all completed when he awoke and there were even more customers already waiting outside the shop! Every shoe fitted every foot perfectly, even though they were all different.

The shoemaker made enough extra money to buy a wonderful meal for his wife along with the materials for the next day.

Just before they went to bed the shoemaker's wife said, "My darling, we have been ever so fortunate to be blessed by whatever magic has made these shoes. Let us stay awake and watch what happens, and then maybe we can somehow thank whoever has been helping us."

So the shoemaker and his wife stayed up and hid behind a big armchair in the corner of the room. They waited and waited and then suddenly, when the clock struck midnight, a dozen little elves came tumbling down the chimney!

They watched in amazement as the elves picked up the tools and the leather and began making the shoes.

When all the work was done the elves bounced back up the chimney leaving behind some of the finest footwear the shoemaker had ever seen!

"We must do something for these elves," said the shoemaker's wife. "They have surely saved our little shoe shop. There must be some way to repay them!"

The shoemaker thought about it for a moment then said,
"Did you see their feet?"
"Yes!" replied his wife. "They weren't wearing any shoes!"
"Perhaps I could make them new pairs of shoes?" said the shoemaker.
"Yes! That's a wonderful idea!" said the shoemaker's wife.
"And did you see those tatty old rags they were wearing? Well, I shall make them some beautiful new clothes to wear instead."

So that very day the shoemaker began making twelve little pairs of shoes while his wife made twelve fine shirts and twelve pairs of trousers.

That evening, when the shoemaker laid out his materials for the next day, he also left out twelve tiny outfits and twelve tiny pairs of shoes. The shoemaker and his wife hid behind the big armchair again and waited for the elves to appear.

When midnight arrived, the elves came tumbling down the chimney again and saw the beautiful presents that had been left for them.

The elves were ecstatic! They cheered and danced and then put on their new shoes and one by one they jumped out of the window. The shoemaker never saw the elves again, but he continued to make beautiful shoes using the secret tricks he learned from watching them. The shoemaker went on to be very successful and his shoes became well known in all the fashionable cities.

# The Witch's Well

Once upon a time, there was a princess who lived in a land where everything was so dry that hardly any food could grow. One day, the king said to the princess, "We don't have enough food in the palace for you to eat. You must leave us now, to seek your fortune. Maybe you can find a way to bring water back to the land?"

The princess left the palace, with only a crust of bread to eat. She walked for miles, through withered forests and dried-up fields. Eventually, she came to a dark and dusty castle. "Perhaps the people in the castle will give me some food," she thought. So the princess knocked on the door.

The door was opened by an old woman, wearing a blue dress and a pointed hat. "Come in, my dear," she said. As soon as the princess stepped into the castle, the huge door slammed shut behind her. "You are my prisoner now," said the old woman, who was really a wicked witch. "You must work for me."

The princess was forced to sweep the floors of the castle and bring the witch all the horrible ingredients to put into her cauldron. From dawn until dusk, the princess slaved for the witch and at night, she was forced to sleep on a bed of straw in the cold courtyard. No matter how hard she dusted and swept, nothing in the castle ever seemed to get clean.

In the middle of the courtyard was an old well. The witch had forbidden the princess to go anywhere near it. However, one night, she heard a small voice that seemed to come from inside. "Help me!" it called. So the princess crept quietly over to have a look.

"Please, help me," called the small voice, again. It was coming from the bottom of the well. The princess could not see who the voice belonged to, so she lowered herself down in the old bucket that used to draw water from the well. Down and down went the bucket, until it was far from the surface.

The well was so deep, the princess could hardly see the opening above her. At the bottom, there was nothing, except a little toad. "Please, help me!" said the toad. "I am a prince who has been enchanted by the witch and trapped down here. The only way I can escape is by swimming up through water, but the witch has drained the well of water."

"And I am trapped in the castle," said the princess. "I cannot free you." "There is a way," said the toad. "The witch cast a spell to suck the water from this well, and all the land around, into a magic bottle. She keeps the bottle by her bed and if you can get it, we can use it to free ourselves and restore the land to life again."

"I will try to get the bottle," said the princess and she pulled herself up out of the well. She crept silently across the courtyard, so as not to wake the witch. Then the princess curled up on her straw bed and thought about how to get the bottle that held all the water of the land.

Every day, the princess tried to find a way to sneak into the witch's room in the tallest tower. But the witch kept the room locked and the only time it was open was when the witch was asleep.

One night, the princess climbed to the top of the tower and crept into the witch's room. The witch was fast asleep and snoring. The princess opened a wooden chest near the bed. She took out the magic bottle and put it in her pocket. However, as the princess opened the door to leave, it creaked loudly.

Suddenly, the witch sat up in bed. "How dare you enter my room!" she screeched. The witch jumped up, grabbed the princess and pulled her downstairs and across the courtyard to the well.

The witch made the princess climb into the bucket, then she lowered it to the bottom of the well and cut the rope. "Now you're trapped, forever," shrieked the witch. "You can stay down there with that slimy toad."

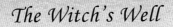

The princess began to cry. "We'll never escape now," she sobbed. "Don't worry," said the toad. I have a plan. Did you get the bottle?" "Yes, said the princess. "I put it in my pocket before the witch woke up." "Uncork it," said the toad. "And be ready to swim!"

The princess pulled the cork out of the bottle. Suddenly, all the water of the land gushed out. It soon filled up the old well and the princess and the toad floated to the surface. The water carried on flowing. It filled the courtyard of the castle and spilled over the turrets, flooding the dusty, dry land all around.

# The Witch's Well

The witch heard the noise and opened her chest to find that the magic bottle was gone. She ran down from her tower in a rage, but a great wave carried her out of the castle far, far away and she was never seen again.

The waters seeped into the baked ground and the earth was no longer parched. Soon, everything began to grow and the land was green and fertile once more.

The curse on the toad was lifted and he became a noble prince once again. When the princess saw him, she fell in love with him.

The prince and the princess returned to the princess' palace, where her parents greeted her with joy. The prince and the princess were soon married and lived happily ever after.

# Beauty and the Beast

Once, there was a poor merchant who had three lovely daughters. The youngest daughter was the kindest and most beautiful. Her name was Belle and she loved her father dearly.

One day, when the merchant had to go on a long journey, he asked his daughters what presents they would like him to bring back. The older sisters asked for dresses and jewels, but Belle knew that her father was poor and could not afford such finery. "I only want a rose, Father," she said.

The merchant journeyed far and wide. On the way back to his village, he was caught in a tremendous storm. Seeking shelter, he found a glittering palace. Nobody seemed to be in the palace, not even the humblest servant. Every one of the huge rooms was empty. The merchant sat down to rest and saw that a table was being magically laid for him. The plates and food flew through the air, as if they were being carried by invisible hands. The surprised merchant ate a hearty meal, then decided to continue on his way.

As he was leaving the palace, he saw a rose bush and remembered his promise to Belle. The merchant reached out and picked a single, red rose. Suddenly, there was a crash of thunder and a horrible beast appeared.

The beast had a bristly, hairy head like a wild boar's, with big teeth. Its hairy arms dragged on the ground, yet it wore clothes like a man. It snorted and snuffled. "How dare you steal from me!" cried the beast, in a rage. "Is this how you repay my hospitality?"

The merchant said he was very sorry and explained that he was only picking the rose for his daughter. But the beast wouldn't be calmed. "To pay for your crime, you must send this daughter to live with me. If you do not, I will come for you and take your life!"

The merchant hurried home and told his family what had happened. "I must go to the beast, or it will kill you," said Belle, sadly. The merchant wouldn't let Belle leave, but that night, she climbed out of her bedroom window and walked all the way to the palace, by herself.

The beast was waiting for her. At first, Belle was terrified by the sight of such an ugly monster, but the beast bowed and welcomed her politely. The invisible servants prepared them a delicious meal and they ate together. "This palace is your new home," grunted the beast. "There are many delights for you here. And now, I have a question to ask you. Will you marry me?"

Belle was shocked. "I can't marry you. I've only just met you," she said. The beast didn't look angry. He just nodded sadly and left.

That night, as Belle slept, she dreamed of a handsome prince. The prince seemed to be calling to her. "Save me! Please save me!" he cried.

The next day, Belle explored the palace. It was beautiful and magical. The invisible servants fetched her any food and drink she asked for. Every room was filled with beautiful dresses, gold and jewels and all manner of fine objects. When she was bored, the invisible servants would carry her through the palace in an armchair. It was almost like flying!

Every evening, Belle and the beast would eat together and the beast would always ask Belle the same question. "Will you marry me?" But Belle always refused. Even though she couldn't dream of marrying such a hideous monster, she grew to love the beast. He gave her anything she asked for and in return, she was able to soften his rough manners and calm his dreadful temper.

Every night, Belle dreamt of the handsome prince. "How can I save you?" she would ask, but the prince would only say, "Don't trust appearances." There was something about the prince's eyes that reminded her of someone. But try as she might, she couldn't think who it was.

As the months passed, Belle began to miss her family. One night, she asked the beast if she could visit them for a while. "I cannot refuse you," said the beast. "But I love you so much, if you do not return soon, I shall die." The beast gave her a magic ring which transported her back home to her father and sisters.

Belle was so glad to see her family that she spent many days in their company. She almost forgot about the palace and the beast, until one night she had another dream. This time, it was the beast she saw, lying in the palace, almost dead from grief. "I have been so cruel!" cried Belle. She touched the magic ring and, in a flash, it transported her back to the palace in the blink of an eye.

Belle ran down the marble corridors and found the beast, just as he had been in her dream. He was lying on the floor, unmoving. She ran to him and cried, trying to wake him up. When her tears fell on his bristly face, he opened his eyes. "It is too late for me," he said. "I think I am going to die. Goodbye, Belle. It's a shame you didn't want to marry me."
"I will marry you, beast!" cried Belle, hugging him tightly.

The moment she said the words, Belle felt the beast begin to change. He stumbled away and turned from her and when he turned back, he was no longer a beast. In his place was the handsome prince from her dreams.

The prince smiled at her. "I was cursed by a wicked witch to be a beast," he explained. I have lived alone for many years, too afraid to go into the outside world because of my ugliness. "The only way to break the curse was to find someone pure enough of heart to marry me, even though I was so horrible to look at."

Suddenly, ll the servants became visible around him and they cheered the happy couple. The prince used the magic ring to bring Belle's father and her sisters to the castle. Soon after, the prince and Belle were married and they lived happily ever after.

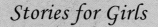

# The Fisherman and his Wife

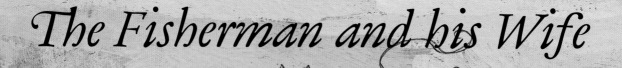

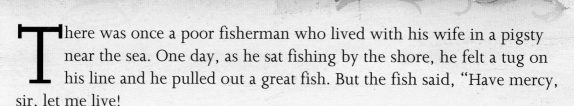

There was once a poor fisherman who lived with his wife in a pigsty near the sea. One day, as he sat fishing by the shore, he felt a tug on his line and he pulled out a great fish. But the fish said, "Have mercy, sir, let me live!

I'm not really a fish at all, but an enchanted prince. I beg you, let me go!" The fisherman gasped in surprise, but he did as the fish asked.

When the fisherman returned home he told his wife how he had caught a fish, and how the fish had told him he was really an enchanted prince so he had let it go. "And you asked for no reward in return for his life?" asked the wife. "Go back and tell the fish we want to live in a snug little cottage."

The fisherman didn't like to ask for a reward, but he was afraid of his wife, so he went to the seashore, where the water was calm and blue, and said:

> "O great fish in the sea!
> I beg you, won't you listen to me?
> My wife Isabill
> Must have her own will,
> And has sent me to claim a reward from thee!"

The great fish came swimming to the surface and said, "Well, fisherman, what does your wife desire?"

"Oh!" said the fisherman. "My wife doesn't want to live in a pigsty she wishes for snug little cottage instead."

"Go home, then," said the fish. "She is in the cottage already!"

So the fisherman went home, and in place of the pigsty was a snug little cottage, with his wife standing at the door.

"Is this not better than the pigsty?" she asked, sweeping her arms around the cozy room. And the fisherman had to agree that indeed it was better.

"Now, we shall be happy!" he said.

## The Fisherman and his Wife

And so they lived happily for a few weeks, and then one day the wife said, "Husband, there is not enough room in this cottage. I should like to have a large stone castle to live in. Go back to the fish and tell him we'd like a castle to live in instead."

The fisherman didn't like to ask for another reward, but once more he was afraid of his wife, so he went to the seashore, where the sea looked sickly yellow and green. And so he stood at the water's edge and said:

> "O great fish in the sea!
> I beg you, won't you listen to me?
> My wife Isabill
> Must have her own will,
> And has sent me to claim a reward from thee!"

"Well, what does she want now?" asked the fish.
"Oh!" said the fisherman. "My wife wants a large stone castle now."
"Go home, then," said the fish. "She is in the castle already!"

## The Fisherman and his Wife

So the fisherman went home, and in place of the snug cottage was a large stone castle. Inside the castle the rooms were all furnished with silver chairs and silk carpets. His wife said, "Is this not fine?"

The fisherman had to agree that it was, and said, "Now we shall be happy!"

The next morning the fisherman was woken early by his wife, who said, "Husband, look outside the window. I should like to be King of all that land. Go back to the fish and tell him I'd like to be King."

The fisherman didn't like to ask for yet another reward, but even now he was still afraid of his wife. So he went to the seashore, where the sea was dark and muddy, and the surface was broken by large waves. He stood a little way back from the water's edge and called:

"O great fish in the sea!
I beg you, won't you listen to me?
My wife Isabill
Must have her own will,
And has sent me to claim a reward from thee!"

"Well, what does she want now?" asked the fish.

"Oh!' said the fisherman. "My wife wishes to be King of the land as well."

"Go home, then," said the fish. "She is King already!"

So the fisherman went home, and as he approached the castle he saw that it was guarded by a troop of soldiers, and inside he saw his wife sitting on a golden throne with a crown of rubies upon her head. And his wife said, "I am King. Is it not great to be King?"

And the fisherman had to agree that indeed it was great to be King, and said, "Now we shall be happy!"

But the wife had not been King for more than an hour before she said to the fisherman: "Husband, it is not enough to be King, so I wish to be Emperor as well. Go back to the fish and tell him I'd like to be Emperor.

The fisherman really didn't want to ask for yet another reward, but now his wife was King, so he couldn't refuse. So he went to the seashore, where the sea was black and full of violent waves. He stood quite a way back from the water's edge and cried:

>"O great fish in the sea!
>I beg you, won't you listen to me?
>My wife Isabill
>Must have her own will,
>And has sent me to claim a reward from thee!"

"Well, what does she want now?" asked the fish.

"Oh!" said the fisherman. "My wife doesn't wish only to be King, she wishes to be Emperor as well." "Go home, then," said the fish. "She is Emperor already!"

So the fisherman went home once again, and as he walked up the red carpet in the great hall he saw his wife sitting on a huge throne made of diamonds and pearls, with a cloak of mink around her shoulders. And the wife said, "I am Emperor. Is it not tremendous to be Emperor?"

And the fisherman had to agree that indeed it was tremendous to be Emperor, and said, "Now, we shall be happy!"

But that night the fisherman's wife could not sleep. "For all my power as Emperor," she thought, "I do not have the power to make the sun rise in the sky." This vexed her a great deal, and so she woke her husband to speak with him.

# The Fisherman and his Wife

She said, "Husband, go to the fish once more and tell him I must be lord of the sun and the moon."

The fisherman was horrified by his wife's demands, but now his wife was Emperor and must be obeyed. So he went to the seashore, where he saw that the the waves were as tall as mountains and threatened to sweep him into the sea. And so he stood far from the water's edge, and shouted:

> "O great fish in the sea!
> I beg you, won't you listen to me?
> My wife Isabill
> Must have her own will,
> And has sent me to claim a reward from thee!"

"Well, what does she want now?" asked the fish.

"Oh!" said the fisherman. "My wife wishes to be lord of the sun and the moon."

"Go home, then," said the fish, who had finally had enough.

"You'll find that it is a pigsty again!"

And there they live to this very day.

# The Magic Mirror

Once upon a time, there were three sisters who lived with their godmother in a tumbledown cottage. The two younger sisters, Constance and Clementine, were always arguing with each other and making mischief. Their older sister, Clara, spent all her time trying to teach them to be good.

One day, the sisters' godmother called them into her parlour. "You are all old enough to know the truth now," she said. I am a good fairy who swore to take care of you after your parents died." I am your Fairy Godmother and I have a special gift for you."

The three sisters watched in amazement as their godmother showed them a beautiful mirror with a delicate, silver frame and a strange, murky surface. "This is a magic mirror," said the Fairy Godmother. "Any girl who looks into it will see the man she will one day marry."

The girls were all very excited. "Let me try it!" cried Clementine, grabbing the mirror. She gazed into it and saw herself with a poor soldier. His clothes were ragged and his sword was rusty. He was begging for money by the roadside.

Clementine laughed. "I would never marry such a man!" she scoffed. "Why, I have a grand duke who is in love with me. I will marry him."

Sure enough, some time later, Clementine did marry the duke. However, her new husband loved to gamble. One night, he bet all his money, his great house and his land, on a roll of the dice. The duke's luck was poor and he lost everything. He had to become a soldier again and he and Clementine were forced to beg for money in the streets, just as the mirror had shown.

Meanwhile, Constance had also looked in the mirror. It showed her living in the house of a poor shoemaker. "I don't think so!" said Constance. "A fine earl wants to marry me, not some silly shoemaker."

Constance was worried by what the mirror had shown her, so she married the earl as soon as she could. The day after their wedding, the earl brought Constance to a tiny shop in the middle of town. All kinds of shoes were in the window. "I am only a poor shoemaker," he said. "I told you I was an earl to get you to marry me."

Constance was very angry at her lying husband. "You rogue!" she cried and chased him around his shoemaker's shop. The magic mirror had shown the truth and Constance had to live as the wife of the poor shoemaker.

The eldest sister, Clara, hadn't looked in the mirror. She loved a woodcutter, who lived in a small cottage in the middle of the forest. He brought firewood to their godmother's house every day and he always remembered to pick a bunch of flowers for Clara.

One day, Clara was curious to see if she would indeed marry the woodcutter. She picked up the mirror and stared into it. The mirror showed a vision of Clara in a sparkling wedding dress, walking down the halls of a magnificent palace, where a handsome prince lived.

"That can't be right," Clara said. "I want to marry the woodcutter, not a prince. I don't care how rich he is, or how big his palace is. It's the woodcutter I love."

The Fairy Godmother had been watching Clara. "The mirror never lies," she said. "Do what your heart tells you and everything will be all right."

Soon, the woodcutter asked for Clara's hand in marriage. "I do not have much money," he said. "I am afraid that your life will be a hard one." "I have your heart," said Clara, "And that's all the treasure I need." She tried not to think about the picture she had seen in the mirror.

"Come with me," said the woodcutter, smiling. Instead of taking her to his cottage, in the middle of the woods, he took her down a different path. At the end of it, a fine carriage was waiting for them.

The woodcutter pulled off his worn-out rags to reveal fine garments underneath. He helped Clara to climb into the carriage and it took them far away, to an enormous palace. "I am a prince," explained the woodcutter. "But all the fine ladies I met only liked me for my riches. I pretended to be a woodcutter to find a girl who was pure of heart. When I met you, I knew that you were that girl."

Clara was overjoyed. She would have been happy with the woodcutter, no matter what, but finding out that he was a prince made her happier still. The mirror had shown the truth, after all. "If only my family were here," Clara sighed sadly.

The next day, three carriages rolled up to the palace, which was beautifully decorated for the wedding. Constance and her shoemaker husband were in one carriage, Clementine and her soldier were in another and the Fairy Godmother was in the third.

"You must all come and live with us," announced the prince. "We have all the riches that you need." Everyone rejoiced, they were happy to accept the prince's generosity.

Clara and the prince had a magnificent wedding. None of the sisters ever needed to look in the magic mirror again, because each one of them had found perfect happiness.

# Wilfred Wolfred

**W**ilfred Wolfred was a Big Bad Wolf. Well, he used to be until he turned over a new leaf and became a medium-sized good wolf instead. Wilfred Wolfred was having a Big Bad Day.

It all started when he got out of bed and stubbed his toe on the table leg. It got worse when he went to make toast and found the bread was stale. And then it got worse and worse. By mid-morning he had lost his handkerchief when he went out for a walk. And by lunchtime he had torn a hole in his best shirt!

Wilfred wondered what he had done to deserve such bad luck, especially since he had been good all week long . . .

On Monday he heard that Mrs. Red Riding Hood was having trouble with her plumbing. So, now that he was a good wolf, he gathered his tools and went to help her.

"I'm so glad to see you!" cried Mrs. Red Riding Hood. "There's a hole under my sink and the water is flooding my kitchen."

Wilfred Wolfred took his tools and after much huffing and muttering he managed to mend the hole in the pipe. All his huffing made Mrs. Red Riding Hood's daughter a little nervous, for she didn't know that Wilfred Wolfred was now a good wolf. But Wilfred barely thought about gobbling her up at all as he was so busy under the sink.

# Wilfred Wolfred

On Tuesday he'd promised to help Mrs. Little Pig repair her roof. He tried not to puff too much as he mended the thatch on the roof, for fear of it blowing down again. Mrs. Little Pig's sons were supposed to help him, but he couldn't find them, so it took him a long time to fix the roof. Her sons were hiding from Wilfred, as they didn't know that Wilfred Wolfred was now a good wolf. But Wilfred certainly was not going to blow the roof down again after his work to fix it.

On Wednesday he got a phone call from Mrs. Goat. Her grandfather clock was going wrong and kept chiming all the time and waking her kids up. Now Wilfred was feeling rather tired, but since he was now a good wolf he forced himself out of bed and went to help. Luckily it was only a white mouse that was stuck inside it, so he didn't have to stay too long. This was a great relief for the seven little goats, as they were sure that Wilfred Wolfred was going to gobble them up. But Wilfred was too busy stopping himself from thinking how the mouse might make a tasty mid-morning snack to worry about them.

# Wilfred Wolfred

On Thursday he went for a walk. As he passed underneath a very tall tree he heard cries. Stuck at the top of the tree was The Boy Who Cried Wolf. Even though he was very hungry and wasn't at all sure the boy was really stuck, Wilfred climbed up to help. And though his mouth watered, and he could have easily gobbled up the boy without anyone noticing, he didn't.

Now, here he was on Friday having a Big Bad Day. He'd done nothing but good deeds all week, and yet he was having the worst luck. He felt very annoyed. What was the point of being good if bad things happened to him?

# Wilfred Wolfred

"Maybe if I go back to being bad, good things will happen to me?" he thought to himself. And that's exactly what he set out to do!

First of all he decided to pay Mrs. Red Riding Hood a visit. When he peeked through the window he saw that she was busy taking something out of the stove, so he crept around the other side, where he saw Little Red Riding Hood. She was all by herself in the garden.

So he crept behind the bush, and was just about to pounce, when . . .
"Ah, Wilfred Wolfred, the very wolf I wanted to see!" came a voice
Wilfred stood up quickly, looking sheepish. Well, wolfish.
"Oh, good afternoon, Mrs. Red Riding Hood," he replied.
"I was just coming to find you. I've made you a chocolate cake to thank you for helping me mend my leaky sink," she said.

So Wilfred wolfed down a huge piece of the cake and thanked
Mrs. Red Riding Hood.

"Lucky I didn't eat her daughter," he thought to himself. As after all, there is nothing more delicious than chocolate cake.

# Wilfred Wolfred

Even though a nice thing had happened to him, Wilfred still felt he should do something big and bad. After all, he had changed back now. So he decided to pay a visit to the Little Pigs' house.

Mrs. Little Pig was inside the house sewing. While she wasn't looking he crept into the garden where the three tasty brothers were sleeping in the sunshine. His mouth watering, he was just about to pounce, when . . .

"Ah, Wilfred Wolfred, the very wolf I wanted to see!" came a voice.

Wilfred stood up quickly, looking very red-faced.
"Oh, good afternoon Mrs. Little Pig" he replied.
"I was just coming to find you, to see if you needed any sewing done and to thank you for helping me fix my roof," she said.

So Wilfred went to get his best shirt with the hole in it, and thought how lucky it was that he hadn't gobbled up her sons, or his shirt would never have been mended.

After that he decided to pay a visit to Mrs. Goat.

He was just on his was way when . . .

"Wilfred Wolfred!" shouted a voice. It was the Boy Who Cried Wolf, running towards him.
"Oh, here comes a tasty snack," thought Wilfred, "I get to be bad at last!"
He was just about to pounce, when he saw something. The Boy Who Cried Wolf was holding his handkerchief.
"I saw it from the top of the tree," he panted. "I wanted to return it as a thank you for saving me."

Wilfred Wolfred thanked the boy, for he was very fond of that handkerchief.

## Wilfred Wolfred

He was just about to set out again to Mrs. Goat's house to be really big and bad, when he thought about all the nice things that had happened that day. His tummy was full of chocolate cake. His best shirt had been mended, and his handkerchief had been returned. And his toe hardly hurt at all any more. His big bad day was actually turning out rather well. And it wasn't because he had done anything big and bad, it was because of the good things he had done.

So, then and there, he decided to turn back into a Big Good Wolf. And he would never think about gobbling anyone up ever again. Well, hardly ever.

# Snow White

Long ago, there lived a king and queen who were overjoyed when they had a beautiful, baby girl. However, soon after the child was born, the queen died. The poor king was heartbroken. He held his baby daughter and looked at her. She had lips as red as blood, hair as black as night and skin as white as snow. "I shall name you Snow White," said the king.

A few years later, the king married again. Snow White's stepmother was beautiful, but also very cruel and vain. She was secretly a witch, who had great powers. The new queen owned a magic mirror, which answered any question that was asked of it. Each day, Snow White's stepmother always asked the mirror the same question, "Mirror, mirror, on the wall, who is the fairest of them all?"

The mirror always replied with the same answer, "You, my queen are the fairest of them all."

This made the queen very happy. Secretly, she was jealous of Snow White and feared that the girl would grow to be more beautiful than herself.

One day, when Snow White had grown into a young woman, the queen asked the mirror her usual question, "Mirror, mirror, on the wall, who is the fairest of them all?"

This time, the mirror replied, "Snow White is the fairest of them all."

The queen flew into a jealous rage and decided to get rid of Snow White, once and for all. She summoned a huntsman. "Take Snow White into the forest and kill her!" she commanded. The huntsman didn't want to kill Snow White but, like everyone else in the castle, he was terrified of the wicked queen.

That night, the huntsmen grabbed Snow White from her bed, while she was sleeping, and took her into the dark, dangerous forest. Even though the huntsman was cowardly, he wasn't evil and he couldn't kill Snow White. Instead, he put her down safely in the middle of the forest and warned her not to return to the castle.

Snow White wandered through the forest all night, getting more and more tired and frightened. As the first light of day broke through the twisted trees, she found a strange little cottage. She knocked, but nobody answered. Entering, she found seven little plates around a table, with seven little chairs. and seven little beds in the corner. Snow White was so tired, she lay on a bed and went to sleep.

When she awoke, Snow White saw seven dwarfs staring at her. At first, the dwarfs were angry that Snow White had come into their home. However, when Snow White explained her troubles, they said that she could stay. So Snow White lived in the little cottage with the seven dwarfs.

Meanwhile, the evil queen asked the mirror if she was the fairest of them all. "Snow White is the fairest of them all," replied the mirror. The jealous queen was furious and asked the mirror where Snow White was. The mirror told her about the little cottage, deep in the forest.

The queen used magic to disguise herself as an old woman. The next day, when the dwarfs were working, the queen went to the cottage with an armful of pretty clothes. "Try this pretty dress on, my dear," she cackled. Snow White tried the dress on, but the queen laced it up so tightly that Snow White could not breathe. She fell to the ground and lay still. The queen fled before the dwarfs could return. She was sure that Snow White was dead.

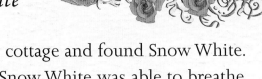

That evening, the dwarfs returned to the cottage and found Snow White. They quickly unlaced the deadly dress and Snow White was able to breathe again. The dwarfs were relieved that no harm had come to their friend.

That night, the queen questioned the magic mirror again, only to find out that Snow White was still alive. This time, her rage was terrible to see. She enchanted an apple, so that one side was full of deadly poison, but the other was safe to eat. The only thing that could break the spell was a kiss from Snow White's true love.

The next day, the queen returned to the cottage, in the magical disguise of a different old woman. "Have a bite of this tasty apple," she said. But this time, Snow White was suspicious and wouldn't touch it. "Look," said the queen, eating the side of the apple that was not poisoned. "See? It's tasty." Snow White took a bite from the poisoned side of the apple and fell down, as if she was dead.

This time, when the dwarfs returned, they couldn't wake Snow White. "She's dead!" they shouted. The dwarfs were very sad. They made Snow White a magnificent glass coffin and cried as they laid her in it.

Long years passed and the dwarfs guarded the coffin every day. Snow White stayed as beautiful as ever, as if she were only asleep.

One fine day, a handsome prince passed by the coffin. "Who is this beautiful girl?" he asked. "I must kiss her." He opened the coffin and kissed the girl's cheek. As he did, Snow White awoke. True love's kiss had broken the curse.

The prince took Snow White to his palace and they were married straight away. Snow White asked the seven dwarfs to join them and they all lived happily ever after.

# The Fox Prince

Once upon a time, a princess named Arabella lived in a palace with her mother and father, the king and queen. The kingdom they ruled was very small and poor. Although the palace was made of marble and had many large rooms, the king and queen could not afford to keep many servants.

One day, a strange man came to the palace. He wore a wide hat with a yellow feather in it and a long, green cloak that reached down to his feet. He had a group of nine red-haired men with him. They also wore big cloaks and wide hats, so that nobody could see their faces clearly. They came into the palace and smiled at everyone. "I am Prince Reynard," said the man, bowing to the king and queen. "I bring you good news. Great riches will come to you."

The king was suspicious. "He doesn't look much like a prince to me," he whispered to the queen.
"Oh, but I assure you I am," said Prince Reynard, who must have had very good hearing. "I travelled to see you because I heard a legend about your palace. It is said that a great treasure is buried deep in the cellars of this castle. To reveal the treasure, everyone in the palace must gather in the cellar. Then, as if by magic, the treasure will appear."

The queen was very excited. "We are in great need of money," she said. "What harm can it do to try this?"
"It sounds very silly to me," said the king, "but if it brings us treasure, who am I to complain?"

So the king ordered everyone in the palace to gather in the Throne Room, ready to find the treasure.

As the king, the queen and the servants walked down to the cellar, Princess Arabella saw that Prince Reynard was hiding something beneath his cloak. It was big and bushy and had a white tip. "That looks just like a fox's tail," thought Princess Arabella! "Look, Mother," she said to the queen. "Prince Reynard has… "

"Not now, dear," interrupted the queen. "We're far too busy."

Arabella didn't want to go into the cellar. She ran and hid behind a curtain and watched as everyone else climbed down the steps. She noticed that Prince Reynard and his men stayed behind.

When the last person had gone into the cellar, Prince Reynard looked around quickly, gave a sly chuckle and promptly slammed the cellar door shut. He turned the key in the lock, so that the people of the palace could not get out. Prince Reynard jumped in the air and clicked his heels together. "Hooray!" he said. "My cunning plan has worked, my fox brothers, the palace is now ours."

Suddenly, Arabella realised that Prince Reynard wasn't a man at all. He was really a big, red fox, standing on its hind legs. His nine men threw off their cloaks and they were foxes, too. "Three cheers for the Fox Prince!" cried the other foxes and they carried the Fox Prince to the Throne Room.

Arabella tiptoed over to the cellar door, but the Fox Prince had taken the key. She spoke to the king through the keyhole. "Help!" called the king from inside the cellar. "There's no treasure! We're trapped! You must get the key, Arabella. Then we can chase the foxes away. But it won't be so easy to fool them, they are cunning beasts."

The foxes were all over the palace. They left muddy pawprints on the beds. They went into the kitchen and carried off the tastiest food. They opened the henhouses and chased the chickens. They frightened the horses in the stables and swung on the chandeliers.

Prince Reynard lounged on the throne, with the king's best crown on his head, while his fox servants brought him the daintiest dishes from the kitchens.

In the meantime, Arabella had thought of a plan. She walked into the throne room, where the foxes were dancing and drinking the palace's finest wine. "Hello, great Prince," said Arabella.

"Seize her!" cried the Fox Prince. "Put her in the cellar with the others."

"Wait," said Arabella. "I have a puzzle for you. But I don't think you're clever enough to solve it."

The Fox Prince was suddenly interested. He held up a paw to stop the other foxes grabbing the princess. He was a very proud fox and didn't like being told he wasn't clever. "I can solve any puzzle," he said. "Tell me what it is, princess."

Princess Arabella took a big, deep breath and told the foxes her puzzle. "In this palace are ten fine brushes that would clean up the mess you have made," she said. "But no matter where you look, they will always be behind you. If you can find them, I'll go into the cellar. If you can't, you have to let everyone out."

The foxes searched the palace, sniffing in every corner. But they couldn't find the brushes. "You're a liar," said the Fox Prince, after he returned to the throne room. He was panting from his search. "There are no such brushes." Arabella laughed. "The brushes are your own tails, you silly foxes!" The Fox Prince felt behind him for his tail and laughed. "You win, princess," he admitted. He held out the cellar key for her.

Arabella took the key from the Fox Prince and ran to the cellar door. She unlocked it and the king and his servants quickly chased all the foxes out of the palace and into the woods. As the Fox Prince left, Arabella thought she heard him cry, "Goodbye, Arabella. It was a pleasure to be outfoxed by you!"

The Fox Prince never returned to the palace and the king, the queen and Arabella, lived happily every after.

# The Ugly Duckling

Once upon a time, in the shady reeds by a river bank, a mother duck sat on top of her eggs. She had been waiting a long while for them to hatch and was getting impatient. Soon, there were cracking sounds, as little ducklings emerged from their shells. One by one, the eggs hatched, except for one. The remaining egg was much larger than the rest and its shell was grey.

Finally, the big egg cracked and a duckling emerged. It didn't look at all like the other fluffy little ducklings. It was big and clumsy and instead of being a beautiful yellow color, it was a dirty grey. It had wide feet and a long neck. Even the mother duck didn't like the look of it.

When the other birds in the farmyard saw the big duckling, they laughed and laughed. "It's the ugliest duckling we've ever seen!" they said. The mother duck and her little ducklings agreed that the strange duckling was just too ugly to have around. The hens pecked him and the turkeys chased him. No one loved the poor little ugly duckling.

One day, the ugly duckling was so fed up that he decided to leave the farmyard and find some new friends. He waddled down to the river, where some wild ducks had landed. "Perhaps they will accept me," the duckling thought and he swam over to them.

Suddenly, there was a loud cracking noise. Before the ugly duckling could speak to the ducks, they flew away in fright. Nearby, hunters fired their guns. They were looking for birds to shoot and their hunting dog was crashing through the reeds. "He'll eat me up!" thought the terrified duckling. But the dog ran right past him.

"I'm even too ugly for a dog to eat!" thought the duckling. He hid in the reeds, with his head bowed, waiting for the hunters to pass.

The ugly duckling swam down the river, until it reached a little cottage near the river bank. The door of the cottage opened and a stern-faced old woman came out, followed by a red hen and a black and white cat.
The woman saw the ugly duckling and grabbed hold of it. "Look Hen, look, Cat," she said. "Now I shall have duck eggs for my supper."

Days passed, but the duckling didn't lay any eggs. "What use are you if you can't lay eggs?" said the hen.
"Can you purr, or catch mice, or arch your back, like me?" asked the cat.
"No, I can't," admitted the little duckling.
"Then you're useless!" said the cat and the hen agreed.

The duckling was just as miserable in the cottage as he had been in the farmyard. "I don't belong here," he said, sadly. "I want to go back to the water." The hen and the cat looked at him and laughed.

"What a stupid idea," said the hen, clucking her disapproval.

"You really are a very silly bird," added the cat.

One day, when no one was around, the duckling waddled outside and swam off down the river again. In the distance, he saw some beautiful swans flying across the sky. The ugly duckling had never seen such magnificent birds and his heart rose at the sight of them. "I wish I could be with them," he thought sadly. But they would never want to spend time with someone as ugly as me. I wish I were as lovely as they are."

Winter came and the weather became colder. The ugly duckling sat in the reeds, shivering and alone. The days and nights grew colder and colder until, eventually, the water froze over.

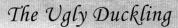

# The Ugly Duckling

While sleeping one day, the ugly duckling was grabbed by a farmer and taken into his house. "This will make a good pet for my children," said the farmer and he put the duckling on some straw by the fire.

However, even though the farmer's house was warm and dry, the ugly duckling wasn't happy. The farmer's children teased him and chased him around the house. He flapped his wings to escape and knocked over a jug of milk, then he toppled over a basket of eggs on the table. The farmer was so cross, he blamed the little duckling and threw him out of the house.

The poor little duckling had nowhere to go, so he hid in the reeds and waited for the long, dark months of winter to pass. Snow and ice covered the land and everything was frozen.

Very slowly, winter turned into spring and the little duckling felt warm rays of sunshine on his back. The ice began to thaw and the snow began to melt. Once again, the river flowed and the duckling was able to swim. Now, however, he found that he could swim faster than before. He had grown too, and his feathers had changed color.

One day, the beautiful swans flew down and landed on the river. Even though he was scared of being pecked and laughed at, the duckling decided to speak to the birds. "I don't care if they laugh at me," he thought.

The duckling swam up to the swans. "I'm just an ugly duckling," he said, sadly. "Please don't laugh at me or peck me, I only want to speak to you,"

The swans looked at each other in amazement. "Look down into the water," said one swan, softly. The ugly duckling looked down at its reflection for the first time that spring. Instead of a gawky, grey bird, it was amazed to find a beautiful white swan staring back at it.

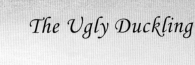

"I'm a swan!" he cried and curved his long, slender neck in joy. The other swans were very happy to have met their new friend. "Fly with us, brother," they said and they all took off into the sky.

The ugly duckling had changed into a beautiful swan. His time of unhappiness and misfortune was over and, at last, he had found his true brothers and sisters. The swan lived a long and happy life and was never lonely again.

# The Little Mermaid

F ar beneath the clear blue waves, the Little Mermaid lived in her father's kingdom with her five sisters and her grandmother. She was the youngest of her sisters, and the loveliest of them all. Her beautiful voice carried far across the water as she sang happily to herself.

More than anything else, the Little Mermaid loved to listen to her grandmother as she told tales of the world above the sea. She was mesmerized by her grandmother's descriptions of human beings and their ships, of the birds that flew high in the sky and the busy towns by the seashore. But it would be some years before the Little Mermaid could discover these things for herself; for a mermaid had to be fifteen before she was allowed to rise to the surface to see these extraordinary sights.

One by one, as they reached their fifteenth birthday, the Little Mermaid's sisters made the journey to the world above the ocean and came back with wonderful stories of what they had seen. The Little Mermaid longed to see these things for herself and waited impatiently for her fifteenth birthday.

On the day she turned fifteen, she could barely contain her excitement as she held on to her sisters hands and they started to swim towards the surface.

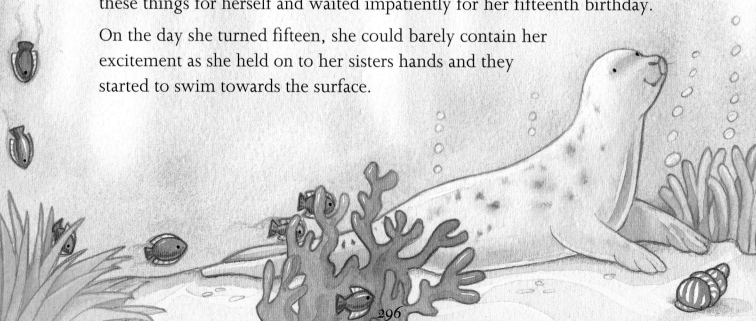

As her head popped above the waves for the first time, the Little Mermaid gasped – for the sun's rays glittered on the water and the clouds glowed pink and gold. It was the most beautiful thing the Little Mermaid had ever seen.

Suddenly, the peaceful scene was shattered by a loud explosion. There before her was a ship, lit up by fireworks in the sky. Laughter drifted across the water. On board the ship a party was under way to celebrate a young Prince's birthday. The Little Mermaid watched as the humans danced on the deck. She gazed at the handsome Prince and imagined herself twirling around in his arms.

As the celebrations went on, the calm seas gave way to waves. They were gentle at first, but the wind grew stronger and soon huge waves were crashing onto the decks of the boat. With a terrifying groan, the deck split in two and the ship began to break up in the swirling waters.

# The Little Mermaid

The Little Mermaid watched in horror as the handsome young
Prince was thrown into the churning sea. At first he swam against
the waves, but soon he grew tired and slipped beneath the surface.
Down, down, down he sank.
"I must save him," cried the Little Mermaid. With a flick of her tail,
she dived beneath the heaving waves and scooped up the young man
in her arms.

The Prince was heavy and at times the Little Mermaid feared she
would never reach the surface, but finally the waves parted and the
Little Mermaid felt the wind on her cheeks once again. She held
the Prince tightly in her arms and allowed the waves to carry them
towards the shore. Just as the first rays of the sun peeped above the
horizon, the Little Mermaid felt sand under her tail.

The little Mermaid stayed with the Prince on the beach for as long as
she dared, singing to him softly. But as the sun's rays grew stronger,
she knew that she had to return to the water.

# The Little Mermaid

The Little Mermaid could not stop thinking about the handsome Prince. Every day she sat on the rocks in the bay to watch him walking in the palace gardens. At first this was enough, but after a while she longed to speak with him.

"But that will never happen," she sighed. "I'll never be human."

"You could be, if you wanted," said a voice next to her. The Little Mermaid turned to find herself face to face with a Sea Fairy. The Little Mermaid hesitated. Sea Fairies were always trouble! But then again, she did seem to know of a way that the Little Mermaid could be human . . .

Ignoring her doubts, the Little Mermaid followed the Sea Fairy.

"I have a potion that will change your tail into legs so you can walk with your Prince," cackled the Sea Fairy. "If you can make him fall in love with you before the sun sets on the second day, you will become human forever. If you fail, you will become a mermaid once more, but must serve me for all eternity!"

The Little Mermaid nodded her agreement as the Sea Fairy passed her a small bottle containing the powerful potion.

The Little Mermaid swam slowly towards the surface with the potion bottle held tightly in her hand. Finally she reached the shore, and sat on the sandy beach below the palace on the cliff. With trembling hands, she uncorked the potion.
It smelled terrible!

Shutting her eyes, she put the bottle to her lips and quickly drank the liquid. Her throat burned and her eyes watered, but it was soon forgotten as the Little Mermaid saw her tail change before her very eyes into two pale legs. Very slowly, she stood up and took her first wobbly steps.

Meanwhile, at the palace, the Prince was gazing far out to sea, thinking about the mysterious girl who had rescued him.
"All I can remember is that she had a beautiful singing voice," he told his servant. "If only I could find her. I long to hear her voice again."

Just then, the Prince's servant spotted a bedraggled girl walking up the cliff path. "She must be a survivor from the shipwreck," cried the Prince. "Bring her into the palace and take care of her." He did not recognize the Little Mermaid.

The Little Mermaid was overjoyed to be invited into the palace – especially when she found herself sitting next to the handsome Prince at dinner. But her happiness was short-lived. For at the meal she heard something terrible. A princess from the nearby kingdom was arriving the next day. The Prince's parents wanted him to marry her.

With a heavy heart, the Little Mermaid retired to her bed. It seemed that tomorrow she would have return to the sea to spend her days serving the Sea Fairy.

As dawn broke the next day, a fanfare announced the arrival of the Princess's ship. The Little Mermaid watched from her balcony as the sails grew larger on the horizon. As the ship got nearer, the Prince prepared to sail out to meet his very special guest.
"Come with me," he asked the Little Mermaid. "I would like you to meet her."

The Little Mermaid made her way down the palace steps and climbed aboard the boat. The boat skimmed across the water and soon it was alongside the Princess's ship. Seeing the Princess, the Little Mermaid was filled with dismay.

She was very beautiful. Her dark, silky hair shone in the sunshine and her eyes sparkled as she gazed at the Prince. The Little Mermaid was certain she had lost her Prince forever!

# The Little Mermaid

Celebrations lasted for the rest of the day, but the Little Mermaid could not join in. How could she celebrate, when her Prince was to marry another? Soon the sun would dip behind the horizon, and she must return to the sea to become a slave.

Suddenly the Little Mermaid heard a splash. She looked up, it was her sisters! "All is not lost," they told her, when they heard their sister's tale. "We heard the Prince's servant say his master longs to hear the voice of the girl who rescued him. You must sing, sing with all your heart!"

So, as the sun began to set, the Little Mermaid sang the song she had sung to the Prince on the beach. The haunting melody drifted across the sands to where the Prince was standing. At once, he rushed over to the Little Mermaid and embraced her.

"It was you who saved me," he cried, planting a kiss her on her cheek. "I have searched for you everywhere! I will never let you go again!"

Just at that moment, the sun dipped behind the horizon. The spell was broken and the Little Mermaid's wish had come true – she would be human forever and stay with her handsome Prince!